I AM
PRISCILLA

I AM PRISCILLA

From Passover to Pentecost

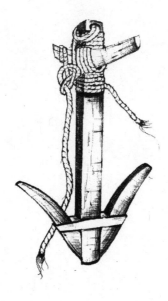

Book Two in the Passover Trilogy

Lon A. Wiksell, D. Min. & Ryan Wiksell

Foreword by Barri Cae Seif

Published by Our Father Abraham

KANSAS CITY

www.ourfatherabraham.com

ISBN: 978-1-7323705-4-8

Wiksell, Lon, 1949—

I Am Priscilla : From Passover to Pentecost / Lon A. Wiksell, D.Min.

Cover design by Ryan Wiksell and Kara Wiksell

OUR FATHER
Abraham

Our Father Abraham is a ministry of Lon A. Wiksell, D.Min. The organization's mission is to be a vital resource for people of all backgrounds to understand the Hebraic roots, and essential Jewishness, of the Christian faith.

Our Father Abraham accomplishes this through teaching, worship, advocacy, and celebration of the Jewish Sabbath and other festivals.

Visit our website at: **www.ourfatherabraham.com** to learn more.

For Haddon, Simeon, Asher, Anya & Teodora

May the God of Abraham, Isaac and Jacob
keep you and bless you. And may you love
him with all your heart, soul, and strength.

Table of Contents

FOREWORD

Prepare to be taken on a journey! Dr. Lon Wiksell and Ryan Wiksell adeptly weave this beautiful story, using the biblical narrative as a backdrop to produce a truly inspiring work.

As a woman, I have always enjoyed the true story of Priscilla and Aquila, which is found in Acts and in the letters of Paul. It was when I saw the movie *Paul the Apostle* that I first came to appreciate her character. Priscilla strikes me as a very sharp woman, skilled both in running a business and in teaching the Word.

Lon and Ryan bring this striking woman forward in their narrative, as they weave her life together with the Spring biblical feasts of ADONAI. As you, the reader, progress through this work, expect to learn lessons from the Bible that could apply to your own life.

Regardless of your gender, I believe you will enjoy this book, as it offers a beautiful story as well as great biblical instruction.

Barri Cae Seif, Ph.D.

Theologian and Professor of Bible and Business
Intimate Moments with the Hebrew Names of God
The Name – HaShem: Daily Devotional Worship
Is Christ Really the End of the Law?
www.barricae.com

INTRODUCTION

I Am Priscilla: From Passover to Pentecost is the second book of the Passover Trilogy, by Dr. Lon Wiksell and Ryan Wiksell. In the first book, *The Last Seder of James,* John the Apostle comes to Jerusalem to share a Passover Seder with James, the brother of Jesus, in prison on the night before James is martyred. Although it is only hinted at in the first book, one of John's traveling companions, and the chronicler of that story, is a legendary teacher of the first-century church named Priscilla.

This book follows the story of Priscilla as she and her fellow believers cope with James' execution, and count the fifty days from Passover to Pentecost. The narrative begins on the first day of Passover and proceeds for seven weeks (referred to in Jewish tradition as the Counting of the Omer.) During these weeks, Priscilla recounts eventful journeys by land and by sea, the results of a devastating series of earthquakes, an encounter with a slippery heretic, and a miraculous work of the Spirit on the day of Pentecost. In the process she and her companions wrestle with important questions—concerning motherhood and barrenness, Jewish and Christian identity, the delay of Jesus' promised return, and what it really means to be his hands and feet here on earth.

This introduction provides basic background information about the premise of the story, the characters, the setting and the Jewish traditions of the Counting of the Omer and Shavu'ot (also known as Pentecost). The story itself comes next, presented in the format of a fifty-day personal memoir, divided into seven weeks. As such, the action develops, unfiltered, before Priscilla's own eyes, and the reader experiences it all in the present tense.

After the Story section comes the Teaching. This begins with a series of lessons about the characters in the Story, as well as the historical and biblical significance of the Counting of the Omer and Shavu'ot (Pentecost) traditions, first to Judaism, and then to Christianity. All information provided after this is for reference, including a glossary of Hebrew terms, a brief selection of relevant Scripture passages, author bios and a list of resources for further learning.

I Am Priscilla presents a unique arrangement of both fictional and non-fiction material, which does not follow the pattern of other books to which the reader may be accustomed. Thus, there is no one "right" way to read it. Instead, the authors invite each reader to enjoy this book his or her own way.

The Passover Trilogy

Of the seven biblical festivals outlined in Leviticus chapter 23, three of them carried expectations of pilgrimage. As commanded in Deuteronomy 16:16, all Jews who were able to travel to Jerusalem did so for the festivals of Passover, Shavu'ot (Pentecost) and *Sukkot* (Tabernacles). These three are referred to as the Pilgrimage Festivals, and form the basis of the trilogy.

The first book, *The Last Seder of James,* is focused on the festival of Passover. This, the second book, is about Pentecost, and the Counting of the Omer leading up to it. The third book, entitled *Seventy,* will feature the Feast of Tabernacles, alongside the other fall festivals (primarily Rosh Hashanah and Yom Kippur).

Although the first book is the only one to feature Passover explicitly, the themes of Passover (such as Creation, Exile, Deliverance, Covenant, and Redemption) define the trilogy as a whole. The three-part narrative thus proposes that all the Jewish festivals are built upon the foundation laid by Passover. This is how the three books came to be known as the Passover Trilogy.

The Story

This book picks up where *The Last Seder of James* leaves off. The first chapter, entitled "Passover", is a retelling of the finale of the first book, told through Priscilla's eyes. As the story progresses, Priscilla travels back to Ephesus with John and company, encounters a persuasive heretic, and wrestles with personal disappointments. In time, she joins the Ephesian church in coping with a mass in-migration of refugees seeking relief from natural disasters.

A tradition of the Jewish people (outlined in Leviticus 23:15-16) is to count the fifty days after Passover, culminating in Shavu'ot (the Feast of Weeks), also known as Pentecost. This practice, called the Counting of the Omer, frames the story of the book, as Priscilla keeps a daily journal of the events in her life throughout this seven-week period.

As in the Counting of the Omer itself, this story points forward to a narrative climax on the day of Pentecost.

The Characters

In the development of character, every effort is made by the authors to adhere first to the words of Scripture, and second to the lessons of history and archaeology, such as they're known. Although the reader may discover some minor departures from the latter, any deviations at all from the former are unintentional and open to correction in future editions.

Ultimately, these characters are developed far beyond the limits of both Scripture and History. This will naturally occur in any work of historical fiction, but there is a deeper purpose. It is the authors' desire to help the reader identify with these characters as people just like us. When reading Scripture, it is all too easy to view the characters as "wholly other", almost alien beings. In reality, they walked through their lives from one day to the next just as we do, working hard, loving their families, making mistakes and trying to find meaning in the world.

The more we, as students of Scripture, can learn to see its characters through this lens, the more we stand to benefit from the reading. Below is a brief introduction to the main characters found in the story. For more detailed profiles, turn to page 147.

Priscilla

Although Priscilla is only mentioned six times in Scripture, a few biographical facts are clear. She was a tentmaker, a preeminent teacher of the first-century church (and namely of Apollos), the wife and ministry partner of Aquila, and a trusted associate of the Apostle Paul.

For the sake of this story, one assumption is made about her life and work: that Priscilla was the author of the biblical epistle to the Hebrews. Although this is by no means certain, it is grounded in credible literary and archaeological research. This, of course, expands the potential trove of background data for Priscilla's story. It gives her a voice, a legacy and a core teaching. It also fleshes out her biographical profile as an authoritative figure in the church of Rome, even long after she and Priscilla relocate to Corinth, and eventually to Ephesus.

More detail about the letter to the Hebrews, and questions of its authorship, can be found on page 157.

Even when the case for the authorship of Hebrews is granted, many questions remain. Was Priscilla born Jewish, converted Jewish, or simply a well-read Gentile? Where and when was she born? Was she a first-person witness to the ministry of Jesus? These and other questions are explored in her detailed profile on page 147.

Aquila

Aquila is never mentioned in the Bible apart from Priscilla. Therefore, everything we know about Priscilla from Scripture must also be true of Aquila. The only exceptions are (a) his secondary position, which may imply that he was the less influential member of the couple, and (b) his confirmed Jewish ethnicity and origination from Pontus, in northeast Asia Minor (modern-day Turkey).

4

As a result, the authors have made a number of imaginative presumptions about Aquila—namely in regard to his travels, his leadership and his marriage—which are explained on page 150.

John the Apostle

John son of Zebedee (John the Apostle, John the Beloved, John the Evangelist) was one of the twelve disciples appointed by Jesus. Among the twelve were the sons of Zebedee—John and his older brother James—whom Jesus called "Sons of Thunder". This John should not be confused with John the Baptist (John the Baptizer, John the Immerser) who was Jesus' cousin.

The plot of this story depends, in part, on the past role of John in caring for Jesus' mother Mary. Many have concluded that he relocated from Israel to Ephesus early in his ministry, and brought Mary with him, eventually building her a house on Mt. Koressos, immediately south of the city. John ministers both locally and abroad, as the Spirit leads him. As such, he does not hold a distinct office within any given local church, and wields his outsized influence lightly.

John authored five books of the New Testament: the Gospel of John, the three epistles commonly known as I John, II John and III John, and the book of Revelation. For more about the book of II John, see page 158.

Nicolas / Nicolaitans

The character of Nicolas is built on a series of reliable assumptions, grounded in the mention of a group called the "Nicolaitans" in the second chapter of the book of Revelation. Further description of his character can be found on page 152.

Other Characters

A number of supporting characters in the story are drawn directly from Scripture, such as Apostles Peter and Paul, Gaius, Apollos, Diotrephes and Demetrius. Brief profiles are provided for each, beginning on page 153.

The Setting (Time and Place)

The year AD 62 was a pivotal one in the early community of Believers in Jesus. Some scholars believe it is the year that the letters to the Ephesians and the Hebrews were written. And, as the first book in the trilogy, *The Last Seder of James,* depicts, James the brother of Jesus was martyred at Passover that same year.

History tells us that James' death was the opening salvo in an eight-year period of upheaval in this region of the Roman Empire. Ananus ben Ananus, the high priest who oversaw the execution, was deposed due to the resulting public outcry, and the office of high priest would remain unstable for the remainder of its existence. At that time, Ananus's own son (appropriately named Jesus) began predicting the impending destruction of the Temple. Just two years later, Rome was crippled by a wildfire, which Caesar Nero blamed on the Christians in the city. Before the dust settled, thousands of Christians were executed, including the Apostle Peter. Paul was executed in Rome just a few years after that. In the year 66, a riot in Caesarea sparked a 4-year war between Rome and Judea. In a dizzying series of military episodes, the advantage shifted back and forth until AD 70, when the city of Jerusalem and its Temple were utterly destroyed. These events will be featured in the third book of the trilogy, titled *Seventy.*

I Am Priscilla is a journey narrative, and as such features a wide variety of geographic settings. Priscilla begins in Jerusalem, and subsequently travels along the Jordan River and through the region of Galilee. She then embarks from the city of Ptolemais across the Mediterranean and Aegean Seas, to her home in Ephesus.

The story of Priscilla is comprised largely of fictional events in the city of Ephesus. These events are based, to an extent, on the true historical record of the region, and have been modified for the sake of character and plot development.

To read more about the historical context of the story, see page 154.

Counting of the Omer

The Spring Festivals celebrated by Jews and outlined in Leviticus 23 are strongly rooted in harvest cycles. Passover, in mid-Spring, marks the barley harvest, and begins the countdown to the wheat harvest. In Leviticus 23:15, God commands "Then you are to count from the day after the Sabbath, from the day that you brought the Omer of the wave offering, seven complete Sabbaths. Until the day after the seventh Sabbath you are to count fifty days, and then present a new grain offering to ADONAI."

This new grain offering marks the festival of Shavu'ot, or Pentecost. Thus, for thousands of years Jewish people have counted fifty days from Passover to Pentecost, which is referred to as the Counting of the Omer.

In the story, Priscilla not only observes this practice, but uses the Omer to mark the individual chapters in her story. Read more about this tradition on page 168.

Pentecost and Shavu'ot

As the second book of the Passover Trilogy, *I Am Priscilla* is focused on the Jewish festival of Shavu'ot, or Pentecost. This is one of the seven holidays prescribed in Leviticus 23 for Israel to observe in perpetuity. At its root, Shavu'ot is a celebration of the wheat harvest, which comes seven weeks after the barley harvest, represented by the festivals of Passover and First Fruits.

By the Second Temple period, Jews had come to identify Shavu'ot with the establishment of God's Covenant[1] on Mt. Sinai. Tradition holds that the Children of Israel arrived at Sinai on the fiftieth day after their Exodus from Egypt, thus adding a new layer of meaning to the festival. With this, what had begun as an agricultural observance became something much richer.

---

[1] Exodus 24:3

This association—between Shavu'ot and the Covenant—set the stage for the Great Outpouring of the Holy Spirit, as told in Acts chapter two. The parallels between the two events are nothing less than astonishing, and will be explored in detail in the Teaching section after the story (page 169 and following.)

Suffice it to say that those who understand Pentecost in both the Torah and in Acts can scarcely doubt that the two are tightly linked. What's more, the very fulfillment of the original festival can be clearly seen in the outpouring of the Holy Spirit, from the first century to the present day.

Although Priscilla's story takes place thirty-two years after the Great Outpouring (or the first Christian Pentecost, estimated to have occurred in AD 30) it serves to echo this milestone in the fictional events set forth in first-century Ephesus. While we, as Believers, should not expect the Acts of the Apostles to repeat themselves in our time, we should nevertheless look to the Holy Spirit to move in transformative ways in our own lives.

In other words, Pentecost is more than a past event, and more than an annual festival. Pentecost is an unbroken reality for all who trust in the Spirit of God to renew their hearts—and reshape the world—day by day.

Hebrew Terms

In this edition, Hebrew terminology is kept to a minimum. Wherever Hebrew is important to the Story or the Teaching, footnotes are provided for definitions or other background information. Pronunciation guides and further explanations can be found in the Hebrew Terms section on page 182.

PASSOVER
AD 62

"I am James!"

The introduction came from the top of the wall, across the Outer Court, barely cutting through the roar of the Passover crowd. I aggressively shushed Milos, in the middle of telling another one of his stories. Everyone around us quieted as well, and turned their faces to the east.

"...brother of Jesus the Nazarene!" the words poured forth from a backlit figure with sharp shoulders and a ragged robe whipping in the wind. It was our James—who'd been imprisoned in the Antonia Fortress for a week, and held in custody for over a month now. James is the whole reason we came here from Ephesus, when John received word that he was in trouble. But now my mind was racing with questions. What did his appearance at the top of the wall mean? That our mission had succeeded, or failed? And where was John?

"You know this name!" he bellowed, referring to Jesus. He pointed his finger at the crowd and moved it slowly from right to left as he addressed his audience. "Many have undertaken to spread falsehoods about him throughout Judea, Samaria and the ends of the earth. I am here to dispel these falsehoods." James spoke boldly, but woodenly, as if the words were not his own.

John should be here, I thought again. Wasn't he supposed to have been with James, in his prison cell last night? I hoped against hope that he hadn't been apprehended as well. I wondered if maybe I should go look for him at the fortress after this. But my worries about John were causing me to miss what James was saying.

"You all know that this Jesus was crucified at Golgotha. Some of you stood witness!" *This can't be happening,* We had come here to rescue James, not to attend his funeral. James continued preaching, and I

---

[2] *Nisan* is the first month of the biblical Hebrew calendar (Exodus 12:2)

watched the priests on the wall as their faces went from stern, to nervous, to furious. I heard a group of Pharisee rabbis gathered at the column next to ours. "Go up! Go on up!" they shouted at each other, urging someone—anyone—to ascend the stairs to the wall and put a stop this display.

"I tell you this!" James continued. "Jesus is seated in the heavens at the right hand of ADONAI—our Passover Lamb forever!" *There it is. The sentence that will get him killed. Oh, James!* I cried inwardly, grinding my teeth to keep my composure. I watched in desperation as a handful of the rabbis I overheard a moment before were now gang-rushing James, along the top of the highest wall on the Temple Mount.

My Abba was a Pharisee, and a rabbi. But the Pharisee rabbis at the Temple this morning were not like my Abba. I heard them shouting feverishly, trying to drown James out, while also ordering the Roman guards to shove him off the wall. *It isn't right! Somebody stop them. John!*

The silver-and-red clad soldiers glanced questioningly at Ananus, the high priest, who grimaced and nodded. In an instant they hoisted James' armpits up onto their armored shoulders and marched him away from the crowd as he continued shouting. He closed his eyes just as they heaved him over the opposite ledge, to the valley floor below. He didn't scream or cry out. He didn't make a sound. No one did.

Until, that is, another group of Pharisees (which had been watching him from just below his perch on the eastern wall) began shouting and storming out the eastern gate just a moment later. "Stone him!" they cried, "Stone him! Stone him!" again and again. *Did he not die on impact? ADONAI have mercy. I wanted to cry out and tear my robes, but I was frozen in place, my heart forgetting to beat.*

Once that rioters had left the Temple, everyone who remained was stunned. Nobody moved or spoke. James was precious to the city of Jerusalem, and not only to the Believers in Jesus. Everyone I talked to had a story of James helping them, or helping someone they knew, or advocating for the oppressed, or mourning with the bereaved. What could possess anyone to harm such a man?

We should say something, I thought. *People will listen.* My brothers and sisters were beginning to stare at me. Simon. Jude. Susanna. Thea. They wanted me to do it. But my head was a hive of wild bees, my tongue swollen and seized up like a rusted ship's rudder. I couldn't think. I couldn't speak. Perhaps it's still no excuse. But it was as if I saw it all happening from a distance. We hadn't arrived soon enough to save him. ADONAI, *give me something to stand on! I'm drowning here.*

Just then, another sound of shouting came from the southern colonnade. It was rhythmic and song-like. A psalm? The sound spread, from the south to the east to our own ears on the western edge. Then the words became clear. "Hosanna to the Son of David!" they were shouting.

Hosanna? I couldn't believe it. Who started this? All of us Believers were gathered by the western columns, and it didn't come from us. "Hosanna to the Son of David! Save us, Son of David!" Over and over, the cry for salvation grew from a murmur to a shout to a deafening roar.

I closed my eyes and remembered Jesus' triumphant entry to the City, thirty-two years ago. I remembered the giant palm leaves, robes and tunics paving the road. "Hosanna to the Son of David!" we all exclaimed as the King of Creation paraded by on a sad little donkey. "Save us, Son of David!" We were all in a state of euphoria, believing that this was the moment promised to King David so many centuries ago—that a messiah had come to take up his throne, restoring glory and sovereignty to our people once more.

But it didn't take long for us to change our tune. Less than a week later, those once-faithful enthusiasts were shouting "Crucify him! Crucify him!" and everyone who wasn't calling for his execution had disappeared entirely. The women were all who remained. I was there, too, but at the fringe. Behind Martha and Salome, behind the Marys. Present but terrified.

I snapped back to the present when a raindrop hit my nose. Within moments the sprinkle became a downpour. I heard goats bleating desperately for shelter, and doves flapping violently in their cages.

"Hosanna to the Son of David! Save us, Son of David!" The cries continued, even as the crowd crushed together to fit under the porticoes at the perimeter of the Outer Court. *He's done it,* I exclaimed to myself. *His message broke through.* And through my fear, through my despair, a ray of James' own fiery joy shot through. I shouted Hosanna with the crowd as our souls melded together. On and on and on it went, until finally a piercing shofar[3] blast silenced the crowd.

The third hour had come. My family huddled around me, our faces streaked with the mingled tears of tragedy and triumph. But now their eyes were all asking one question—the same as mine. *Where is John?*

---

[3] Shofar: Trumpet fashioned from a ram's horn

WEEK I

Jerusalem is in total chaos right now. It's the first day of the week—during Passover—so the feast of Firstfruits is in full swing.

I'm sitting in a corner on the ground floor, in the House of Zadok near the Essene Gate. My pen alternates incessantly between writing this, and translating letters for James and Jude. I'm trying to focus on just one or the other—or anything at all—but strangers keep bursting through the door asking for lodging. A divan, a mat, a clean space on the floor—anything. It's not my house, so I can't help them. There are already more people staying here than I can count. (Sorry, that's a figure of speech. I counted eighty-three.)

What a fascinating house this is. It used to be the main community house for the Essenes[4] in Jerusalem, which is why it's situated just inside the Essene Gate, and adjacent to the southern wall. It even has a private entrance for the old *mikvot*[5] just outside the wall. The door was sealed up years ago, but it was probably used by Jesus and the disciples the night of their last meal together. I doubt their Essene hosts would have allowed them into the Upper Room unless they'd used the Essene *mikveh* first.

What's more incredible is that the Essenes allowed them in at all—I gather Jesus made a big impression on them. So they welcomed him with open arms, even when it meant permitting his cadre of non-Essenes to use their rooms. Today it serves as a refuge for Jesus' surviving brothers and sisters—Simon, Jude, *et cetera*—and their extended families.

Yesterday, I wrote about the incident at the Temple. We found John, eventually. He was standing in the valley, soaked to the marrow, just looking up at the Temple. Once we got him into some dry clothes, he insisted we go straight to the Arimathean's tomb, so we could see to

---

[4] Essenes: A Jewish sect which arose in the first century BC and continued till approximately AD 68.
[5] Mikveh: A ritual bath for ceremonial purification. Plural: *mikvot*

James' remains. But since it was the Sabbath all we could do was sit in mourning until sundown. Then some of the women and I unwrapped his shroud, applied our myrrh and aloes to his body, and bound it up with strips of white cloth, almost like a swaddle. Before we finished I lifted his body into my lap, with everyone watching. For one sweet moment he felt like a newborn in my arms. An image flashed before me of Mary rocking her little James gently, with those same arms that held our swaddled Savior. Suddenly I sensed that everyone was watching me, and that I was sobbing again, so I put him down. That is to say, I put *his body* down.

After committing James to his tomb with a prayer of mourning, we shuffled back to the House of Zadok to eat some matzah[6] with Milos, Demetrius and the others. The dinner hall was packed with Believers and ablaze with emotion—shock, grief, praise, and utter disbelief.

What an awful thing—I can't believe James is gone. But oh, the way he went. It happened more than a day ago, and my head is still spinning from that scene—the sermon on the Temple wall, the shofar blasts, the shouts of *hosanna!* that lasted an hour—it felt like the Great Pentecost all over again, but this time in the midst of a horrific execution.

Jude came to where I was sitting, and set some matzah was in front of me, but I couldn't eat. James' execution still felt like a punch to the stomach, and it was affecting John even more. I traveled here with him; I heard how he talked. He honestly believed he would be able to rescue James from death. This is not the first apostle we've lost. It's not even the first *James* we've lost. John's older brother James—also one of the Twelve, and a fellow Son of Thunder—was beheaded by Herod Agrippa eighteen years ago. *Eighteen years? Has it really been so long?*

It's enough to dismantle a weaker faith, if I'm honest. And I've seen some unfortunate souls go that way. Jesus said this generation would not pass away before he returned! What generation, exactly? How many do we have to lose before we see him again? How much oppression do we

---

[6] Matzah: Unleavened bread, especially that which is eaten at Passover

have to undergo? *How long, ADONAI? How long?*

After dinner John and I had a long talk, and he told me about his conversation with James in the prison cell. He went into great detail about it, so I recorded as much as I could. Perhaps we can share the story with the church when we return to Ephesus.

We also prayed—a lot. It was very late when we parted, so I'm exhausted today. (As you can see, my penmanship is horrid right now.) John prayed in the Spirit during most of the first watch, and when he opened his eyes, he told me something shocking.

"Priscilla," he said, and paused for a long time. "Something new is upon us. A new work of the Spirit."

"I feel it too," I replied. And I did feel it.

"He didn't show me what it is. All I heard was 'I am doing a new thing. Watch and see.'"

"Just watch?" I asked.

"And write. You, my sister—write what you witness."

"You want *me* to do it?"

"God wants you to do it."

I was stuck. I've done more than my share of writing, for a woman. But nothing like this. I had so many questions.

"So— should I write about you? Should I follow you around?"

"It's not about me, Priscilla." I furrowed my brow. Was he just being humble? John smiled faintly. "Don't avoid me, but don't make it about me. Count the days, and tell *your* story."

"My story? Why me?" Such a thing had never crossed my mind. I could tell my father's story, peace be upon him. I could tell my husband's story. Or the story of John, or Paul—even Apollos. They all have fascinating stories I would love to tell. But me?

"It's not only about you, of course." John added. "It's about Aquila, about your family in Capernaum, about your students, and your brothers

18

and sisters in Ephesus. All of you."

"Who would even read that?" I blurted out. I'm afraid I sounded cynical, but John didn't flinch.

"I would read it. The church at Ephesus, the church at Rome. Perhaps many others. I've seen your writings before—the stories you tell of Orpah, of Melchizedek, even your father's story. But you also have a story of your own."

John stood up for the first time in hours, then grabbed his feet one at a time, pulling them up behind his back to stretch his knees. "And if you don't think you have a story yet, very soon you will."

"The Spirit showed you that?"

"Yes."

I shook my head in disbelief. A moment later a broad smile came like a reflex. I couldn't help it. What a rush it is, to be told that I am more than a scribe, more than a teacher. I am the protagonist of my own story.

Then, without warning I felt a sudden wave of doubt, and a flood of tears. *Who am I, really?* I pleaded. *Who am I but the plain-faced daughter of a Galilean rabbi, and the barren wife of a Jewish tentmaker?* I felt like Moses, being chosen against all apparent reason. I could ask God to make someone else do it, but I already know how that would turn out. Especially if I start comparing myself to Moses.

John remained still, his eyes closed. At length, he spoke again. "Today is the first day of the Counting of the Omer. These fifty days will be unlike any before them, culminating in a great wind of the Spirit. Open your eyes, Priscilla. See his work, and show it to the nations."

"Oh, John. I want to, but— " My mind struggled for words. (Aquila could tell you how rare this is.) I fidgeted for a moment before finding myself again. "I mean to say—yes. I will. I'll start in the morning."

My name is Priscilla, which means *noble*. My parents named me Avrah, but my husband gave me the name Prisca (which is the proper form of the name) when we moved to Rome, just after getting married. He thought I looked beautiful and stately like the senators' wives, and back then he told me all the time. Now he jokes about how the name Prisca can also mean *ancient,* which is sad but true.

When my husband first moved to Rome—before we met—he changed his name to Aquila, which means *eagle*. His parents named him Abdiel, but he didn't want to sound so Jewish amongst the Roman dignitaries (even though he was there to advocate for the Jewish people.) The eagle is the symbol of the Roman empire, so he thought Aquila was a good choice. I always liked the sound of it, too. But I don't think Abba would have approved.

We lived in Rome eighteen years, but not anymore—not since Claudius expelled all the Jews thirteen years ago. (He didn't have the good sense to exempt Jews like us, with dignified Latin names.) For a while we lived in Corinth, and then moved to Ephesus, where we live now. We like it well enough. It's a big city like Rome, and there's a large community of Believers to gather with.

But right now I'm in Jerusalem, as you know. Last time I was here, it was for Passover and Pentecost, thirty-two years ago. At the time I thought the City couldn't hold another soul. I kept waiting for the walls to burst outward at any moment. But the City proved me wrong. There are more people here now than ever. It invades your sight, your hearing, your every thought. Even the smell is overwhelming.

I keep asking myself why I don't just leave. But I always know the answer. Because this is *Jerusalem*. It's the middle of everywhere. For the first time in decades I get to be in the most glorious city in the world, at the most glorious time of the year. That's why everyone else is here, too.

I've probably thought about my last time here every day since then. Every day for thirty-two years is 11,680 days. That's a lot of days to reminisce. But everyone else I know, who saw Jesus crucified and raised again, is the same way. You never forget, even if you want to.

But how else could it be? To watch the Son of Man suffer death so that, by the grace of God, he might taste death for everyone! And we got to see it with our own eyes. Who could ever escape death if they neglect such an awesome salvation? How *could* we forget?

It doesn't seem like 11,680 days ago. I remember it better than the ship I arrived on last week. (Did it have one sail, or two? Never mind.) But when it comes to Jesus, all I have to do is close my eyes and I'm back there again, at the Cross. At the Empty Tomb.

All of us women, who had been following Jesus—we were horrified and transfixed. We couldn't look away no matter how much we wanted to. His body was bruised and bloodied to the point he no longer looked human. When we slaughtered our lambs for Passover, we did it humanely. But what they did to Jesus was not humane. Not at all.

We just stood there wringing our hands, afraid to get too close. But the men had fled the scene completely—all of them except John, who stood at the periphery as if he could bolt at any moment. It was just unspeakably awful; words have failed me ever since.

But that was the beginning, not the end. At the feast of First Fruits we remember that there is so much more. Jesus may have died as our Passover Lamb, but he has risen as our Great Shepherd. So much that was shrouded in mystery has now become clear as polished silver. That our Savior was both the High Priest and the Perfect Sacrifice. That we had the Lamb of God *with us!* And just as at Passover we are crucified with him, at First Fruits we are raised with him in glory. *Hallelujah, Hallelujah!*

My favorite thing about this house is the murals over the doors, with names of angels and archangels to identify each room. Naturally there's a Michael room and a Gabriel room, as well as a few others that surprised me: Sidriel, Kepharel, Nuriel... who are *they*? I have no idea. The Essenes were really into angels.

I say "were" because the Essenes don't really exist anymore. They formed after the Maccabean revolt to return the Temple and the Priesthood to a state of purity reminiscent of the time of Solomon and his high priest Zadok. (That's why they claimed to be "Sons of Zadok".)

They secluded themselves from all of society, refused to marry, procreate or do business with the outside world. They followed the Torah like a science, immersed themselves multiple times per day, and put all their hope in a soon-coming Messiah. So when that Messiah showed up, and fulfilled the entire Temple system in one fell swoop, the Essenes joined up, almost to a man.

So now the entire Essene quarter—or should I say Essene *corner*—of the city is full of Believers. And the House of Zadok, with the voices of Jesus and the apostles echoing from the walls, sits at the epicenter. So much is different now—most believers get married (God help us!) and a few of us know how to run a business. But there are also some things that never change. As before, life is fully communal. Everyone shares everything; the words *mine* and *yours* are never uttered. And for some reason everyone here is still really into angels.

John surprised me this afternoon. I'm not happy.

"Do you want to stay here, in the city?" he walked up and asked me, as if we were in already in the middle of a conversation.

"What do you mean? Where else would I be? It's only the fourth day of Passover." The city was still so thronged that even the daily business of the crowd outside was deafening. We almost had to shout at each other to be heard, which made it seem like we were arguing.

"I'm going back to Ephesus."

"What? Why?"

"The Spirit is calling me back. I don't know why. Do you want to stay here, or come with me?"

I love John. *The Elder,* they call him. With my whole spiritual being I love having him as a brother. But he's been keeping me off-balance lately, and he won't let me recover. I sighed loudly enough to make my frustration obvious. Of course I wanted to stay. But how was I supposed to write this account he says God wants if he's in Ephesus and I'm here?

"Well, where is this new work happening—Ephesus or Jerusalem?"

"It's your story, dear lady. I suppose your story will happen wherever you are." I dropped my face into my hands, and stayed that way for a moment or two. When I looked up, he was gone.

The sun is high in the sky above us now, and we're headed down the hill to Jericho. (Yes, I went with John. I don't really know why.) We each got a donkey for the journey, which sounds more comfortable than walking, but the slope to Jericho is so steep that I've been tempted to get off this beast half a dozen times. It's a wonder I can even write. My kingdom for a scribe!

The closest and soonest boat to Ephesus departs from Ptolemais, which is a long road trip from Jerusalem. But the good news is that it will take us through Capernaum—my hometown. We can stay with my mother (who I still call Ima) and my sister Hadassah there. Hopefully we can stay two nights instead of one—I haven't seen them in 1,151 days. (Aquila always rolls his eyes at me when I count time in days instead of years. I'll try again.) I haven't seen them in *over three years.*

We write back and forth all the time, but I'm very excited to see them and hug them again. It's almost enough to make up for leaving Jerusalem in the middle of Passover.

Omer 5 | Thursday

We camped beside the Jordan last night. The site could have been
better but the tents were top-notch. (I wonder who made them?) Before
finding a place to settle in, we passed through Gilgal. We might have
stopped there, but John seemed a little stressed about the length of the
road to Ptolemais, and wanted to cover more ground before nightfall.
Gilgal is where our ancestors crossed into the Promised Land. It's also
where John the Baptizer preached and baptized people (including me) in
the Jordan, a lifetime ago.

We went during the final year of the Baptizer's life. Of course we
didn't know that at the time. Abba had just died, and Ima and Hadassah
visited the Jordan with a group of women from Capernaum, on our way
to Jerusalem for Passover.

I'll admit, it was awkward at first, approaching a man in the water. I
was eighteen years old, and—according to Ima and her friends—overdue
for marriage. So I'd never been touched by a man who wasn't a relative,
and wasn't sure what to make of this scene in the Jordan at first. I was
nervous, and he could tell. He didn't touch me—he didn't touch anyone
in the river, actually—and he motioned for me to stop before I came too
close to him.

"My sister!" He shouted so the crowd could hear. His voice was gritty
and thick, like a bear. He looked me in the eye and offered a warm, easy
grin. "What is your name?" he bellowed.

"I am Avrah, daughter of Joash!" I shouted back, louder than
necessary.

"Avrah..." He switched voices, adopting a thoughtful murmur. "Yes,
your name is Avrah. Mother of a multitude..." he translated, trailing off.
"And so it shall be." Suddenly he resumed his shouting voice. "Bless

ADONAI! Many will call you Mother!"

I startled at the pronouncement, and looked back at my own mother to see her beaming with pride. Apparently, the Baptizer gave another blessing after that but I didn't hear it—I just stood motionless in the river like a dumb stick fallen from a tree. If he hadn't motioned for me to cross my arms, hold my nose and lower myself into the water, who knows how long I would have stayed frozen there?

I don't talk about this memory much. As I wrote before, I have no children. Not only that, I'm fifty-two years old. (At least I've grayed slowly. A strand here, a strand there—I could probably pass for forty-seven.) I don't know why I still cling to this hope. I'm older than every new mother I've ever known. On the other hand, I'm still much younger than Elizabeth was when she gave birth to the Baptizer himself. And younger than Sarah when she had Isaac. I sometimes think of Hannah and her prayer of thanksgiving for the upside-down ways God: "Those who were full hire themselves for bread, but those who are starving are hungry no more. She who was barren has borne seven children, but she who has had many sons pines away." [7]

Where was I? Oh yes. After we were all immersed, Ima, Hadassah and I were soaked and dripping in our double-tunic outfits, like a flock of goats caught in a downpour. But we were grinning and chatting happily about our moment with the great prophet John. We had turned to head up the bank into town when a sound like thunder came from the sky above the river. I say it was "like" thunder, but it was different. It was a ripping sound, like the sound of a thousand angels tearing their robes at once. A light was shining down on John so brightly he'd become invisible. Then I heard a voice coming from the light, but deep like the ocean. The voice was chanting slowly, *"Hen beni ratzetah nafshi."* Behold my Son, in whom my soul delights. [8]

---

[7] 1 Samuel 2:5
[8] See Psalm 2:7 and Isaiah 42:1

I remember how my mind raced when I heard it. The voice had recited the second Psalm, but with the words of Isaiah added, calling him Beloved.

"Who was that for?" I blurted out to anyone who could hear me.

"ADONAI is declaring John the Messiah!" Hadassah exclaimed, clapping her hands together in front of her face.

"No, no, my daughters. It is not for John." Ima was so wise. She couldn't see or hear any more than we could, but she knew better than us. She still does, even in her failing years.

"But John is the rightful high priest!" I insisted. "He is a Nazirite, born miraculously of Zechariah the priest. Why not John?"

"He said it himself, Avrah. Didn't you hear? 'Among you stands one you do not know coming after me, whose sandals I'm not worthy to untie.'[9] That heavenly voice was for someone else. Someone who had *come to John* for immersion."

"Why would the Messiah come to John to be immersed? That's backwards!" I insisted.

"I don't know, Avrah. I suppose we'll find out."

We're far from Jerusalem now, but Passover continues. So before bedding down tonight we recited the Hillel psalms, much like we did at our Seder four days ago. One in particular always stands out to me:

From the rising of the sun to its going down
The name of ADONAI is to be praised
ADONAI is high above all nations
His glory is above the heavens
He settles the barren woman in her home
as a joyful mother of children. Hallelujah.[10]

---

[9] Luke 3:16
[10] Psalm 113:3,4,9. The Hillel Psalms (113-118) are traditionally sung at Passover.

Who is this psalm for, exactly? Certainly not for me. Yes, my hope is in ADONAI, maker of heaven and earth, but I'll admit I'm not always sure what to expect. Or when to expect it. Maybe tomorrow…

Omer 6 | Friday

The weather was cooler today, and it was downright chilly when we broke camp before dawn this morning. The goal is to arrive in Capernaum by the ninth hour, so we have to find a way to get these donkeys to pick up the pace. We have no way of sending word ahead of us, so heaven forbid we should arrive at sundown, just as the Sabbath is beginning!

By sunrise we were crossing the Jezreel tributary and passing into the region of Galilee. I'm still shaking my head as to why I would leave Jerusalem at such a time as this. At least I'll get to see Aquila again soon—I miss his hugs. And his toothy grin. And his big, fluffy beard.

But first, John agreed to stop for two or three days in Capernaum, where my mother and sisters live, with their families. I was really slow to leave, but now these stubborn donkeys can't go fast enough.

Halfway up the western lakeshore we passed through Tiberias—a brand-new city when I was a girl—then Magdala. Back when I was little and Michal wasn't born yet, the rabbi at Magdala died, so Abba spent a year teaching at their synagogue every week. He had to walk there from Capernaum the afternoon of the sixth day and come back the following evening, since it was too far to walk on the seventh day. He missed a lot of *Erev Shabbat*[11] meals that way; Ima blessed ADONAI when it was over.

It was already the ninth hour when we left Gennesaret behind us and rounded the corner of the lake and turned east, toward Capernaum. *We should be there by now.* The sun was still high in the west, and it was

---

[11] *Erev Shabbat* means "Sabbath eve", which takes place Friday evening.

casting our shadows ahead of us on the road. The donkeys didn't care for it, so we had to keep pulling them back on course.

Our house is built into the western wall of the city, so Hadassah spotted us while we were still a hundred paces off. I could hear her squeal from the window, and a moment later she was on the road with Ima in tow.

"Avrah!" she shouted, waving frantically as if I hadn't seen her.

"Hadassah!" I shouted back, laughing and waving both arms around like a lunatic. We spend so much time apart that every time we're reunited it's like we're eight and six again. "Ima! We're coming as fast as we can!" *These stupid donkeys only have two speeds: slow and stuck.*

Demetrius saw that I was fed up with my noble steed, so he shot me a boyish grin and reached out to take the reins. I did a little hop, and rushed off to greet my ecstatic family. By this time more of them had emerged from the gate: Lemuel (Hadassah's son who runs a shop in Sepphoris), Michal (my youngest sister) and four of her six kids: Ana, Samuel, Manasseh and Joash. The reunion made for quite a ruckus out there on the dusty lakeside road. The sheep nearby were beginning to stare.

"Where's Aquila?" Ima asked. Questions were getting lobbed at me from every side.

"Still in Ephesus."

"Who's that behind you?" Ana asked coquettishly.

"That's Milos. He's got seven fingers." He smiled, flashed them proudly.

"How long are you staying?" Hadassah asked.

"Three days." I blurted out. John shot me a glance. "Two days," I corrected. "And three nights."

"What's your donkey's name?" Joash asked.

"My little man!" I exclaimed. Joash was only three last time I visited, and now he's starting to look like a miniature version of his late grandfather—my father—who is also his namesake. Maybe that's why

28

he's my favorite. "Look how you've grown!" I shouted in his face. He just squinted at me.

"You named your donkey Little Man?"

"No, Joash!" we both giggled, and I tousled his hair. "Don't be silly. His name is Go Go Go. At least that's what I've been calling him." Now everyone was laughing.

Two days is not going to be long enough.

What a delight to be sharing an *Erev Shabbat* meal with my family again. Ima works with such solemnity as she retrieves the candles and candlesticks from the cabinet and places them on the table. She invited me to light them and say the blessing, but I wouldn't miss her blessings for the world.

With her hands shaking ever so slightly, Ima held the oil lamp up to each candle, covered her face with her hands and chanted those familiar words, "Blessed are you, ADONAI our God, King of the Universe, who have sanctified us with your commandments and allowed us to kindle the Sabbath lights."

Omer 7 | Saturday

What starts with candles, ends with candles. I normally don't mind a little writing on Sabbath, but in my Ima's house I try to work as little as possible from sundown to sundown. Now the children are sleeping, and I'm watching the *Havdalah*[12] candles burning down, signaling the end of Sabbath and the beginning of a week full of hope and possibilities.

I do my best to observe all God's commandments, including the

---

[12] Havdalah is the Jewish ritual that marks the end of every Sabbath. One of the primary steps in the process is the lighting of a special braided candle.

command to rest on the Seventh Day. But I'm not good at it. I keep remembering that God's very first mandate to humankind was issued to the very first humans: "Be fruitful and multiply." They may have broken the command not to eat the fruit, but they had no trouble at all being fruit*ful*. Now the earth is full of their descendants. It's true—I have no descendants myself. But in spite of this (and perhaps *because* of this) I pride myself in the fruitfulness of my work.

Maybe that's why I have such a hard time putting the pen down when the Sabbath candles come out. And why I'm so eager to pick it up again when the *Havdalah* candle is lit.

WEEK II

Omer 8 | Sunday

Almost every time I look over at John today, he's smiling and shaking his head. I don't think he's accustomed to big noisy families. It's not like we're neglecting him; my family is very aware of John the Elder—John the Apostle—and they have loads of questions for him too. But he grew up with no sisters and just one brother, and he tells me his home life was always orderly and calm. That might surprise you, since Jesus nicknamed the two brothers "Sons of Thunder". I've seen John in a state of passion—righteous rage, even—but normally he's cool as a winter fig. Even under pressure. Especially under pressure.

I'm writing this after dinner, and as I look up I see my niece Ana out in the courtyard having a lively conversation with Milos. She's only fourteen; I hope she realizes she'll probably never see him again after tomorrow. But right now he appears to be telling her the story of how he lost his left middle finger, and almost bled to death in the street before John saved his life. She's spellbound one moment, and giggling shamelessly the next.

"I feel sorry for people like you, Ana, with all those extra fingers," I hear him joking, like always. "Because I have the *perfect number.*" (You know, because seven is the number of perfection.) It's not a funny joke, but she laughed anyway. I'm starting to think they would actually be cute together. Oh well.

Omer 9 | Monday

Hadassah and I are both night-owls, which is fortunate. Otherwise we'd find no time to catch up, with all these kids around. After the little ones went to bed, Ima, Michal, Hadassah and I sat around for a couple hours talking about family, the house church, the marketplace, Ephesus, Aquila—all the important stuff. I told them about John and James, and they insisted I read some of my account out loud to them, which was a little embarrassing.

At first, all four of us were engaged in conversation, but eventually it happened like it always does. Hadassah and I started venturing off the topics normal women talk about, and into the realm of *midrash*.[13] Ima stuck around to listen quietly, like usual. She can't really keep up, especially at her age, but I think our exchanges remind her of Abba.

When Hadassah and I were coming up, Abba always talked about the misfortune of a rabbi to have no sons. "If I'm not going to have any sons," he announced defiantly, "I'll teach my daughters like sons!" Actually I think he taught us harder than sons. After all, if a woman is going to get any respect as a religious thinker, she's got to be able to outsmart the men by a long shot.

So Hadassah latched on to my recitation of James' last Seder,[14] and started asking impossible questions. Fortunately, that's my favorite kind. "Did James bear false witness by agreeing to the Priests' plea deal?" she demanded.

"Does every person deserve true witness?" I countered.

"Well, what kind of person deserves to be deceived?" she shot back. (You can tell you're in a good debate when it's nothing but questions back and forth.)

"What about the person whose very identity is false?" I proposed. Hadassah frowned at me, then smiled. That was my queue to press forward. "The Temple priesthood has become a Hellenistic charade—a puppet regime. As a result all priests are guilty of misrepresentation and collusion with pagan authorities. What *true* testimony can be given to a

---

[13] Midrash is a uniquely Jewish practice, mostly among rabbis, of interpreting Scripture through creative dialogue. Its purpose, according to scholar Wilda C. Gafney, is to "reimagine dominant narratival readings while crafting new ones to stand alongside—not replace—former readings."

[14] A Seder is a liturgical meal for the celebration of Passover. See the first book in the Trilogy, *The Last Seder of James,* to learn more.

false judge?"

Hadassah smirked. "You still believe John the Baptizer was God's true high priest, don't you?"

"Don't *you?*"

"Perhaps..." she said slowly. "Either way, there's no doubt left about the identity of the ultimate High Priest—"

"—in the order of Melchizedek."

"Yes!" We both laughed joyously, before remembering all the sleeping souls around us. I grabbed her ears and kissed her forehead. She rubbed my arms and flashed me her happiest smile.

Abba taught his daughters to find great joy in *midrash,* which would make us popular with rabbis if we were men. But we're not, so we have to keep it to ourselves if we want to have any friends at all.

Omer 10 | Tuesday

Our road is now a crow's-fly from Capernaum to Ptolemais. Around lunchtime Milos got tired of talking about Ana. After a few hours' break, he resumed his questions, but about me this time. "So, what happened to your father?" he asked tentatively. There was a sweet empathy in his voice—poor Milos. He's had it worse off than I ever did.

"He was a lot older than Ima," I replied. "When I was fourteen he started slowing down pretty badly. He was tired all the time, and complained about headaches a lot. Before that, he'd always served his people with such energy, and taught Hadassah and me the same way. So really, the Abba I knew died three years before his body gave out."

Milos stayed silent. His brow was heavy, as he stared at the road ahead of us. The sea had just become visible, like a string of pearls draped over the distant hills. Just beyond those hills, Ptolemais hugged the shore.

"And you were seventeen?"

"Almost eighteen. He nearly died on my birthday, just after Purim." [15]

"Isn't that the same year you met Jesus?"

"Yes. I don't know if a part of me was looking for a man to cling to—I have no brothers, as you know—but it happened almost simultaneously. I met the Baptizer just months after we buried Abba. And I was there when Jesus was baptized, although I didn't figure out what was going on until later."

"John told me you were one of the Seventy."

"Oh he did, did he?" I twisted around in my seat to wink at John, but he was gazing absently to his left. Milos kept asking questions, but I don't remember the rest of it. My mind had already shifted into the trip ahead; I don't look forward to sea journeys, and I don't want to leave here anyway. Maybe I should just turn around. Every time I visit Capernaum I leave a piece of me behind. This time it was my soul.

I hear my old home crying out for me now, calling me Avrah.

Omer 11 | Wednesday

This morning we enjoyed a short, refreshing walk to the Sea. After an hour we had crested the final range of hills, and Ptolemais came into view. The air felt cool and salty as a maritime breeze kissed our cheeks and filled our nostrils. Two hours later we walked through the city gates of Ptolemais, and learned that our ship was still out at sea.

By lunchtime the vessel finally arrived, and the sailors started hurriedly unloading bags and crates into large carts on the dock. They must have been way behind schedule—the captain was barking at them to move faster. I've been on these ships before—the crew is always cranky when there's no time for them to spend on shore. It ruins the mood.

---

[15] Purim, or the Feast of Esther, is an extra-Levitical Jewish holiday to commemorate the defeat of Haman, recorded in the book of Esther.

Omer 12 | Thursday

Our ship embarked yesterday, several hours late but without incident. Despite their grumbling, the crew appears to be working hard to make up for lost time. I wonder what the big hurry is. It's certainly not on my account.

The sun came out late in the afternoon, so I found a comfortable place on the deck to sit and soak it in. For an hour or so I just watched the crew moving back and forth, hoisting sails, adjusting them this way and that. They moved together smoothly, like a graceful animal with thirty-eight arms and thirty-eight legs. But they weren't happy about it. They were speaking Cypriot, so I didn't know what they were saying. But grumbling sounds like grumbling in every language.

One sailor seemed especially aggravated. He was a muscle-bound titan with a big dent in his jaw and an uneven gait. When he spoke, his words came out like the growl of a crocodile. Once I saw the captain give him an order, and the sailor just glared at him. Apparently his mates call him Poseidon, and I can understand why.

Omer 13 | Friday

It's hard to read or write on a ship—almost as hard as on the back of a donkey. The ship is less erratic, but more nauseating. So after a few minutes I have to put the work down. With little else to do, I continued watching the movements of the waves and the crew, while John and Milos were napping down below. I've never been much of a napper, but with the warm sun on my face and the rhythmic sounds of the sea, I actually drifted off for a moment myself. That is, until I heard a warm but husky voice from above my head.

"You must be Priscilla."

"Yes!" I shook my head quickly, trying to remember where I was.

"That's me. Do I know you?"

"That was my hope. My name is Deacon Nicolas."

"Oh! I see. Deacon of…"

"Jerusalem."

"Oh! Of course! You gave a prayer at James' burial. It was beautiful. Unforgettable, really."

"That's me—and thank you. I was glad to contribute, but I regret that we did not have a chance to exchange greetings."

"Indeed. Well—shalom!" I reached out my hand. "it's a pleasure to finally meet you in person."

"Shalom to you, Priscilla. The pleasure is all mine." His eyes sparkled as he reached out for my hand to plant a kiss on my knuckles. "Your name is a good one. Word has reached my family in Pergamum about your teaching. You are the mentor of the great Apollos, are you not?"

I winced a bit. I'd never heard Apollos referred to as "the great" or myself identified as his mentor. "Yes, I suppose so. We knew him in Rome, and in Corinth, and he eventually came to join us in Ephesus. By that time he'd become a powerful orator, but he still had some gaps in his teaching. I was able to fill in those gaps.[16] With the help of my husband Aquila, that is."

"Your *husband,* of course! The handsome Aquila." He made me blush. *What is it about this man?*

"I regret that I have interrupted your basking," he said abruptly. "Please continue, my dear Priscilla."

He made me want to speak with a flourish. "Not at all, Deacon Nicolas. No doubt we'll encounter each other again soon."

I resumed my place in the sun and tried to remember what I'd heard about Nicolas, Deacon of Jerusalem. He was one of the seven original deacons, I knew that much. But as to personal details, I was drawing a blank. After pondering this awhile, I saw him again, across the stern from

---

[16] See Acts 18:24-26

where I was sitting. He was standing alone with the sailor they call Poseidon. The sailor was nodding his head calmly as Nicolas talked. After exchanging a few words back and forth, Poseidon gave him a big, toothy grin. Then they put a left hand on each other's shoulders and with their right they shared a Roman handshake.

Bless ADONAI, I thought. That sailor was starting to frighten me. Perhaps Nicolas has cheered him up. *What is it about this man?*

Omer 14 | Saturday

Another Sabbath is behind us. This time, however, I'm afraid to say we got no rest at all. From morning till dusk we were bombarded with apocalyptic winds, and raindrops the size of grapes. It's nighttime now, but the sky was actually darker *before* sundown. Only in the last hour have I been able to see the hand in front of my face again.

It was not the worst storm I've ever endured, but for most of the day we were terrified the ship would capsize. Rather than push through it, our captain (whose name is Briarus) dropped anchor and prayed to his gods that it would hold. Many times I heard him shout against the wind "Our only hope is in that anchor!" How true that is.

After all, we children of Abraham have a double hope—in the never-changing promise of God, and in the oath that confirmed it. When the storms of life overwhelm us, we reach out for anything to steady ourselves, but the sea floor is too deep. So the anchor goes where we never could, and gives us hope.

WEEK III

Today is the *Lord's Day,* as Gentiles like to say. So we huddled together below deck to sing a Psalm and two hymns while the crew shouted and banged in the background to repair the storm damage from yesterday. Then we took turns reading the Torah portion aloud together. Today's portion was from Leviticus,[17] and not exactly a crowd pleaser.

Ironically, it was my turn when we came to the part about male emissions. So I took a deep breath and read it with as casual a voice as I could muster. But then it was Milos' turn, and the topic shifted to female discharges. "Pass," he said. So Thea read it.

As you can imagine, it was going to be an awkward portion to preach on. So naturally John invited *me* to do it. I talked about how leprosy, and mildew, and all the destructive things in life enter in gradually. Innocuously. Sometimes they're even good things—signs of life. But when we ignore them, they can become deadly. Sin never makes a big entrance. It enters as a mouse in the night, or worse, as an honored guest, arrayed in flattery. I recalled a proverb of Solomon that seemed fitting:

One who hates, disguises it with his lips,
but he stores up deceit within him.
When he speaks favorably, do not believe him,
for there are seven abominations in his heart.

Though his hatred may be concealed by deceit,
his evil will be exposed before the assembly.
Whoever digs a pit will fall in it, and whoever rolls a stone—
it will come back upon him.

A lying tongue hates those crushed by it,
and a flattering mouth causes ruin.[18]

---

[17] Leviticus 14:1-15:33 (*Parshat Metzora,* read on the 16th day of the Omer.)
[18] Proverbs 26:24-28

Saturday's storm had been dramatic enough, but it turned out our high-sea drama was far from over.

This morning, I was speaking alone on the bow with Captain Briarus, and he told me about the repairs to the storm damage. Thankfully, his already-overwhelmed crew had somehow found the energy to replace a dozen ropes, fix the forward mast and patch a huge gash in the upper hull. "But we're lucky," he added. "We only passed through the edge of the storm. Any ship sailing west of here got something much worse."

Before he could say another word, Poseidon—the sailor with the broken jaw—swooped in behind him and clamped his massive right arm around the captain's neck. Then he dragged him straight to the railing, shouting something nasty in Cypriot. In a heartbeat, the First Mate arrived to block him from dumping Briarus into the water, but then more crew members materialized to rally with Poseidon, while others stood frozen along the railing.

In no time it was a full-out brawl. The other passengers and I leapt back from the melee to the left and the right, as the mass of officers and sailors pounded with fists and gashed each other with knives. I prayed furiously, with my eyes pasted open. A few moments later I heard a scream from the crew, and the captain emerged, shredded and panting, but ready for more. Quickly his officers regrouped and surrounded him beside the forward mast. We all stood in suspended animation, as the officers faced off against Poseidon and his allies, waiting for someone to make the next move.

For some foolhardy reason, I decided it should be me. "What good can possibly come of this?" I shouted in Greek at Poseidon. "If you succeed you'll get hard labor for life, or worse. And if you fail you'll be killed!"

Poseidon grimaced at me, his eyes flaming. He turned to square his shoulders with mine, and pulled a long knife from his left boot. Just then,

John, Demetrius and Milos rushed in and planted themselves in front of me, their hands outstretched to deflect the threat.

"Hard labor you say!" Poseidon scoffed, in broken Greek. "I been a slave. As young man I been a slave. Was better than *this!*" He swiped his knife through the air, in Briarus' direction. Then he turned to address his co-conspirators. "You who been slaves—shall we be slaves again?"

"Never!" an invisible face in the group replied. John took a step forward, toward Poseidon. *Bless ADONAI,* I thought. *If anyone can calm him down, John can.*

He took another step forward, then turned right to face the officers. "Captain Briarus!" he bellowed. "You ought to be ashamed of yourself!" We all gasped. *John! What are you doing?*

"These men have followed you tirelessly through savage waters to godforsaken harbors. They have wintered with you and warred with you. And you show your gratitude with brutal treatment like this?" Briarus' jaw was on the deck. He blinked aggressively as if trying to wake from a nightmare. John walked toward the crew, but his eyes never left the captain's.

"Can't you see these men have spent their final ounce? No rest, no diversion, and nothing to eat but battle rations. I ask you, Captain! What else can you expect but mutiny? Shame on you!"

The crew stood taller. Demetrius was tearing up, and Milos was hiding a proud grin. As for me, my mind churned while my heart leapt in my chest. John was casting thunderbolts greater than any storm could produce, and I was starting to understand what he was doing. The officers looked increasingly deflated and angry, and Captain Briarus was on the verge of a breakdown. Finally, it came.

"If only you knew!" he cried, collapsing on the deck and heaving great sobs into his hands. John rushed to kneel beside the captain, and I followed suit.

"My boss in Ephesus!" Briarus cried. "He swore to—" John gripped the captain's shoulder and whispered something into his ear. Briarus inhaled sharply and spoke again. "He swore to break another bone for every day the ship was late. This is the final straw, he said!" A murmur of shock and confusion arose among the crew. Their eyes betrayed a wild array of emotions, from surprise to pity to cold-blooded defiance.

John looked at me questioningly, and I whispered the first words that came into my head. "They don't hate their captain. They need a sabbath."

John nodded solemnly, paused for a breath then stood up to face the crew "Men of Cyprus!" he shouted, scanning their faces slowly. "This crooked merchant in the port of Ephesus has threatened to break your captain's bones. *Noble* men of Cyprus, tell me—would you not stand up for your captain?"

After an excruciating moment of silence, one sailor cried out.

"*I* would protect him!" he shouted, thrusting his fist in the air and leaving it in place.

"Who else?" John asked.

"*I* as well!" declared another, then another.

"It's not our captain's fault we're delayed," said the first sailor. "Look at these storms!" His mates nodded and clamored noisily in agreement.

John turned back to Briarus. "We will pass Rhodes before nightfall. Dock there and give your men a day's leave. We passengers can spare one day, can't we?" The awestruck gathering of several dozen passengers behind us nodded their heads blankly. Anything was better than mutiny.

"Rhodes?" another sailor shouted. "There's nothing good in Rhodes! We would rather be in Ephesus." The crew agreed. John looked to Captain Briarus, then boosted him back to his feet. After a long moment, the captain caught his breath and stood to address the ship.

"It is settled, then. We shall push ahead to our destination. But once we are there, men, we shall take one day's leave."

The crew erupted with cheers of joy, and smiles appeared on every face. Every face but one—the one with the broken jaw.

I looked for Nicolas, but he was nowhere to be seen.

43

Buoyed by the promise of a day off, the crew pushed hard all night and into the morning hours today. By the sixth hour we were in the Bay of Ephesus, and by the eighth hour we were dropping anchor at the massive commercial wharf in the Ephesian harbor. Before the ship could even come to rest, the crew were already tossing crates of merchandise to dock workers, and grabbing bundles of unrefined silk and lumber to load up for the return trip. Our party gathered around John near the gangplank as we waited for it to hit the pier.

Our turn came to disembark, and John led our traveling party off the ship. I felt a tap on my arm from behind, and turned to see Nicolas. This is the first he'd shown his face since the storm.

"My dear Priscilla! You must be overjoyed to finally be home." His eyes twinkled as he smiled warmly at me.

"Indeed I am, Deacon Nicolas. It was quite a journey—especially with that episode yesterday."

"Yes, that was quite a storm," his eyes darted ever so slightly.

"No, that was three days ago. I meant the mutiny attempt."

"Quite right. Well, I have further to go yet. I will be boarding another ship, continuing north to Pergamum. It's been years since I've seen my family there. But I'll spend two nights here in the city," Nicolas added, "as there is no ship tomorrow."

I nodded as we walked side-by-side down the plank. "Will you be returning to Jerusalem?"

"Certainly, after a while. Perhaps for the fall festivals. But I plan to travel back and forth to Ephesus in the meantime. I have many friends in this city, and some business to do."

"What business is that?" I asked.

"I'm a dealer in ropes—all sizes and lengths. You know, that storm of ours was a blessing in disguise, considering how many lines it snapped." He smiled wryly at me, but I'm afraid I just furrowed my brow, like I didn't get the joke. A few steps later we reached the wharf and Nicolas did a double step toward the bathhouses. "Farewell, dear Priscilla!"

I waved brightly, then turned around to see that I was the last passenger off the plank, and the first sailor to step onto it was no less than Poseidon, still scowling. (Granted, it may not be a scowl at all—just his broken jaw.) I shuffled quickly off the end of the plank to give him space to disembark. Then John stepped up behind me.

"Be careful of him, Priscilla."

"Oh I will," I replied. "That man is trouble." A moment later it occurred to me that John may not have been talking about Poseidon, as I assumed. But when I turned to ask him, he had already moved on.

Omer 18 | Wednesday

After disembarking, John headed for the stadium gate with Milos, toward John's house on the hill behind and above the Temple to Artemis. I found them walking through the northern arch after picking up their bags, and bid them farewell, for now. Then I slung my goatskin bag onto my back, and headed up the Arcadian with Demetrius and Thea toward the Amphitheatre, then turned right onto Curetes Way. I said my last goodbyes, and diverted from the main road to skirt around the Agora, till I arrived at our neighborhood, which sits right on the line between the city's rich and poor districts.

I've made up my mind that no city can ever compete with the majesty of Rome, or the glory of Jerusalem. But neither of those cities can be approached by sea. In Ephesus there is a certain exhilaration to cruising through the harbor pillars and suddenly being surrounded by the gleaming marble panorama of Asia's greatest metropolis. With the hubbub of ships flying every known flag, the call-and-response of herons and seagulls—with Mount Pion and the Great Theatre ahead, Mount Koressos and the fabulous hillside villas to the right, and all of it glinting and dappling in the sapphire waters—there's nothing in creation quite like it.

But the Harbor is only the beginning. After disembarking, a stroll up the Arcadian Way—walled in stone and flanked by countless marble columns topped with statues—takes you to the Amphitheatre, which is far larger than it appears from the ship. This monstrosity is cut from the solid rock of Mt. Pion, and they say 25,000 Ephesians can sit shoulder to shoulder on its semi-circular stone benches.

If one were to turn right, pass the Theatre and continue up Marble Way, the Civic Agora is just ahead. This is one of the busiest markets in the Empire, and larger than any piazza in Rome. Continue walking, past the three-story homes of wealthy merchants and dignitaries on the right and the six-story tenements of slaves and laborers on the left, and the 20-cubit fortifications rise in front of you. Once through the gate, you're on the Processional Way to the Temple of Artemis, which locals call the Artemision. Although my feelings about this edifice should be obvious, it's impossible not to be awestruck by the enormity of the structure. I've been to the Parthenon in Athens. That famous temple would look like a modest villa next to the great Artemision. It's simply gargantuan.

The only thing in Ephesus more impressive than the architecture is the people. Although Rome is larger, Ephesus is more colorful. People of every size, shape and hue fill the streets and plazas. Women are given nearly equal berth in the marketplace as men—I know many female landowners, business owners and even some in official positions.

Despite this wondrous variety, two groups of people are painfully ubiquitous: the slaves and the soldiers. For every free civilian seen in the Agora, there is at least one tattooed slave and one uniformed soldier there as well. As people, they are exact opposites—the only thing they have in common is that none of them will look you in the eye. The slaves will not lift their gazes, and the soldiers refuse to lower theirs. We Believers have had some close calls with these soldiers, so we try to keep a low profile. But Pentecost is coming up, and our large gatherings tend to draw the ire of the State. So far, though, we haven't been troubled.

When I arrived at home, I first touched the wooden nameplate to the left of the door, with an "A" on the left, and a "P" on the right, flanking the symbol of an anchor in the middle. I touched the anchor pensively, thanking ADONAI for hope in the storm. Then I touched the stone *mezuzah*[19] on the right side of the door, and kissed my fingertips.

When I entered the house, I found it empty. Aquila wouldn't have expected me home yet, so he was probably out making visits. To be honest, it was nice to have the place to myself for a few hours. After a chaotic festival followed by a wild sea journey, the solitude felt like pure luxury. A little time alone to unpack, and settle down to the idea of living a normal life again.

Omer 19 | Thursday

I must have been even more exhausted than I thought, because I fell asleep on the couch after eating dinner, and didn't see my husband till he woke me up this morning.

"Welcome home, dear wife." Aquila planted a light kiss on my forehead. The morning sun streamed through our second story window. "I'm sorry I didn't see you come in. I was in Smyrna visiting Timothy and his mother.[20] He's still under house arrest, and she's feeling worse all the time."

"Poor Eunice. And poor Timothy. There's no need to apologize, Aquila. I didn't tell you I was returning early." I'm happy to see my husband again, but I keep feeling like I should be happier. Is this what

---

[19] A *mezuzah* is a common ornament on the doorframes of Jewish houses, to remind them of the commandments of God, according to Deuteronomy 6:9

[20] 2 Timothy 3:10-11 reveals that Timothy and his mother and grandmother lived in the distant city of Lystra. It is presumed here that they relocated at some point to Smyrna, which is only a day's ride from Ephesus.

happens after thirty years?

"It's fine, it's fine!" he assured me as he wrapped me up in one of his signature hugs. When he let me go he turned to put some food on a couple of plates—olives, grapes, and generous hunks of bread. "What brought you home? I thought you were staying in Jerusalem through Pentecost."

"I wanted to. But John felt the Spirit calling him back. Either way, my love, it's good to be home."

Aquila smiled warmly, then startled. "I almost forgot! I saw Apollos yesterday, and he said he and Daphne have news for us."

"Oh, Apollos! Is he back now? What was it about?"

"He didn't say; he was in a big hurry. They just got back from Corinth a few days ago. Hopefully we'll see them again soon.

"Right," I replied, still feeling a little blank. Except for the hunger bubbling up as I watched him prepare our meal. "But first things first—let's eat."

———————————

There was very little food in the house, and by the time we'd finished breakfast there was none at all. So I volunteered to go to the Agora and let Aquila rest for a bit. I'd barely arrived at the market when I saw two familiar figures walking in front of me, so I hurried to catch up to them. "Apollos! Daphne!" They turned around and grinned widely, holding out their arms to greet me.

"There's the news!" I exclaimed, gesturing at Daphne's enormous belly. "You're going to have a third! And soon!"

"I know!" she cried. "We're so excited. I hope it's a boy—two girls is enough girls. It's so good to see you, Priscilla! I thought you would be gone longer. When did you get home?" Apollos is one of the most energetic teachers and storytellers I know. He can keep a thousand people spellbound all day long with his parables, anecdotes and teachings. And yet, he's not a talker. Daphne is the talker.

48

"Yesterday," I replied. "Aquila bumped into Apollos yesterday morning and—"

"That's right, love!" she tapped her husband on the chest. "You went to the market twice that morning because I needed more to eat. I'd already had two oranges and about a thousand olives and couldn't get figs out of my mind." Apollos started fidgeting and looked at the ground. Daphne reached out and touched my arm. "Can you *believe* how hungry it makes you?"

"Not really," I muttered under my breath.

"There must be twins in there!" she continued, unabated. She put both hands on her abdomen and left them there. "Castor and Pollux, I'll call them. But those are idols, so how about Jacob and Esau? Do Jewish parents ever name their twin boys Jacob and Esau?" She didn't stop long enough for us to reply. "Then again it could be a boy and a girl—Apollos and Artemis! A boy named after his papa, and a girl after the goddess of Ephesus. But of course that wouldn't work. Two boys would be better. Think of it—two girls and two boys, wouldn't that be perfect?"

I looked Apollos square in the eyes. "I just want you to be happy."

I don't think Daphne even heard me. She embarked down another rhetorical path, talking about everything and nothing that I could possibly remember. I like Daphne; I honestly do. But— well, that's all I really need to say.

Omer 20 | Friday

Today was a quiet day for me to catch up on correspondence while Aquila sat nearby, working on a tent. The church supports us to teach, preach and care for the needy, so we don't need the money from our business anymore. Now we only make tents as gifts, or when a special order comes along.

There was a sizeable pile of letters on my writing table which Aquila had stacked neatly while I was away. I pulled my own work out of my bag—letters from James and Jude to the Church, which they'd asked me to translate from Hebrew to Greek, along with the account you're reading now. Then I turned my attention to the letters. The first three, pulling from the bottom, were unremarkable. But the fourth was catastrophic.

"Aquila, did you read this letter from Rome?" I asked.

"Which one?"

"The one from Junia."

"No, I didn't look at it." He was sensing my anxiety.

Junia had been hosting the church at our house almost since the day we left. The last seven years have been bad ones for the Jewish Believers. But what she had recounted in her letter was simply horrifying. I tried to hand it to Aquila, but he asked me to read it aloud instead. Then he started fiddling with a basket of leatherworking needles—he always needs something to do with his hands when he's nervous.

"'You and Aquila are all too familiar with the trouble we Jews encounter here in the shadow of the Colosseum,'" I read aloud. "'Believers suffer too, so that Jewish *Believers* endure a double share. Worse yet, we *Essene* Jewish Believers receive the greatest of all travails. (I'll never forget your visits when we were imprisoned during the last persecution.)

"'As you know, this house has always been a welcome refuge for those of Essene descent, either by blood or belief. Since your departure, this has become an Essene house to a man, for no other variety of follower will touch us—we are a plague.'" Aquila dropped his materials and rubbed his face. But the worst was still to come.

"'Families have been torn apart, fathers imprisoned or worse, and children apprehended for military training. We cannot care for our widows or orphans, because we are mostly widows and orphans.

"'Thus the Gospel is drying up among us. Instead of spurring us to greater heights of faith, the suffering has walled us in. Prospective Essene believers are joining Gentile churches at best, and avoiding our message

50

altogether at worst. But the vilest danger of all is this: new teachers are appearing from thin air to unravel everything the Apostles have taught us, and scatter us to the four winds. These false prophets are steeped in Essene thought but not regenerated in the truth of our Messiah.

"'Some continue to claim the name of Jesus, but as a *subordinate* messiah. They call him King Jesus, son of David, but put their greatest hope in a priestly messiah who—they say—will come to usher in the new covenant. In the meantime they are appointing themselves interim priests of an alternative temple.

"'Some are denying the humanity of Jesus, saying that he was not born to a woman, but descended upon us as an archangel to teach us a better way. If he was not born, then he did not die. And if he did not die, he did not defeat death and return to life. Instead—they say—he exists forever in spirit form. You know very well the pull that angels have on the Essene mind—the Cross has lost all meaning to those who are being swayed.

"'These first two are corrupting the New Covenant, but there is another group that rejects it altogether. They are casting Jesus in the role of prophet, alongside the Baptizer. *The Second Elisha,* they call him. They are strictly enforcing circumcision, kosher diets and Sabbath regulations, segregating themselves from Roman society to establish a New Israel in the nearby hill country. They do not accept the salvation of anyone outside their creed, and have convinced some of our brothers and sisters that theirs is the only refuge from the terrors of empire.

"'Those unmoved by the falsehoods above are prone to the opposite extreme. For some have come to us teaching what they call Total Grace. For them, Jesus did *indeed* come to abolish the Torah, and replace it with *nothing.* Their message is tantalizing, and sounds godly at first. But the result is only chaos. Men are bringing additional wives into their homes, or worse, abandoning their wives and children in favor of prostitutes. Even some women have fallen prey to this. In the marketplace, greed is the new standard, such that these so-called Believers are viewed as thieves

51

and swindlers, even among pagans.

"'Discussions about the faith are focused on the minute details of interpretation, while the foundational truths are neglected. The hungry, the needy and the stranger are ignored. Leaders like Andronicus and Phoebe, who have persevered in caring for us and teaching faithfully, have been pushed aside to—'"

"Stop!" Aquila cried, jamming the needles back into their basket.

"I'm sorry. It's too much."

"Yes," he whispered. "ADONAI have mercy on us. We are undone!"

I put down the letter and sat on a bundle of orange burlap next to my husband. I took his giant frame in my arms and began to weep. My tears broke his silence, and we mourned openly together. These were our spiritual children, once found, now lost.

We had such dreams for them.

Omer 21 | Saturday

Today is an important day in Ephesus. Nine years ago, on the twenty-first day of the Counting of the Omer, our beloved Mary went to be with ADONAI. The next morning, every Believer in Ephesus paraded solemnly up Mount Koressos from the city, to lay her body in a tomb beside her little home.

Aquila and I had only moved here from Corinth a year prior (along with Paul.) I shudder to think—Aquila and Paul almost missed the chance to know the mother of our Messiah. What a great loss her passing was. It's natural for a church leader to have at least a few enemies, but everyone—Jews, Believers, pagans—everyone loved Mary. And why wouldn't they?

Her presence still hangs in our midst, especially on this day of the year, when the whole assembly of Believers at Ephesus treks up the mountain to bless her memory. That's what we did today.

It was the ninth hour this morning when Gaius and Diotrephes called all the city's Believers to gather at the Agora. Gaius is the unofficial overseer of the house churches all across Ephesus. He's a longtime associate of Paul's and a spiritual hero to many. Diotrephes is the pastor of the city's largest house church, which meets in his home on the hillside overlooking the harbor. He assists Gaius, more and more lately, since Gaius is getting to be quite elderly.

Once everyone was gathered, Gaius stood on a table and gave the benediction in honor of our dear Mary. Then we turned our faces to the south, toward the peak rising above us. Diotrephes took up his walking stick and led the way. After a dozen steps Gaius grabbed him by the shoulder.

"You promise to tell them about the bones?" he asked.

"You really have to ask?" Diotrephes replied with a roll of the eyes. Gaius nodded but Diotrephes didn't notice. Instead he stretched himself as tall as possible and shouted to the assembly with a grin, "First one to the top lights the sacred lamp!"

We all hitched up our bags—stuffed with flowers, anointing oil and provisions for the hike—and followed Diotrephes, although I doubt any of us were determined to beat him to the summit. My fellow travelers from the Jerusalem trip were all there, as well as Aquila, thirty-eight members from our own house church and 424 members from houses across the city and nearby countryside. Every year the group gets larger— I'm amazed at how the community has grown.

Diotrephes has a tradition of reciting Mary's Canticle[21] seven times at various points throughout the journey, and others sing psalms and prophesy. This time, a blessing was recited for the loss of James, especially since he was Mary's son.

Glorified and sanctified be God's great name throughout the world, which he has created according to his will. May he establish his

---

[21] Mary's Canticle, also known as the Magnificat, is found in Luke 1:46-55.

kingdom in your lifetime and during your days, and within the life of the entire House of Israel, speedily and soon; and all say, Amen. [22]

As I recited the Mourners' Prayer with my Jewish brothers and sisters, a fresh wave of sorrow for my brother poured over me like a jar of oil. James brought the kingdom so close we could taste it on our tongues. We could close our eyes and see Jesus descending to the Temple, full of light. What's more, James looked so much like his brother, we could see it with our eyes *open* as well! But now, ADONAI only knows what will happen to the Church at Jerusalem. All we can do is pray.

After that we lifted our voices to sing the Songs of Ascent, [23] and dreamed of Zion.

Those who sow in tears will reap with a song of joy! Whoever keeps going out weeping, carrying his bag of seed, will surely come back with a song of joy, carrying his sheaves."

As the hike proceeded the group became increasingly spread out along the path. The lanky Diotrephes forged ahead with great energy, but not everyone had his speed. Gaius, for one, found the incline more difficult than in years past, and leaned on Apollos more than ever. Some energetic hikers hustled to stay close to Diotrephes. But John, Xanthe, Demetrius, Aquila and I hung back with Gaius and listened to his stories as we walked.

Nearly two hours after leaving the Agora, the last of us in the procession arrived at the peak of Mount Koressos. Diotrephes looked insolent, as if he had been waiting all morning for us.

"John, would you share Mary's story with the assembly?" Diotrephes asked cordially. It was a formality.

---

[22] The "Mourner's Prayer" excerpted here is commonly known in Jewish tradition as the Mourner's Kaddish, one of the most cherished liturgical prayers in Judaism.

[23] The fifteen Songs of Ascent come from Psalms 120-134. These brief Psalms were sung in the Temple services, and by travelers as they ascended the road leading to Jerusalem for Passover or other festivals.

"I think Apollos should tell it," John replied. This is what happens every year, so Apollos was ready. He was not one of those closest to her during her life, but he had absorbed every detail from hearing John tell it privately. Apollos never forgot the details of a story, and once you've heard him recount it, you'd never forget them either.

After Apollos held us spellbound for half an hour, Diotrephes stood on an outcropping and followed the story with a speech. "We Ephesian Believers are heirs to a great and glorious heritage! It is a privilege to remember, so atop this holy mountain we bear witness to that divine calling: to commemorate the holiest of all women, our beloved Mary." A murmur of *amens* cascaded through the gathering, from front to back.

"It is no small duty to steward the sacred remains of our Savior's own mother. The bones beneath this very rock cry out to us, calling us higher and farther, beyond ourselves and our petty humanity, into a truth that can only come from God." *He's not going to say it, is he?*

"We Ephesian Believers have a destiny! Just as our beloved Mary gave birth to God incarnate, we—her spiritual sons and daughters—are called to give birth to a new kingdom. First to Ephesus, then to Asia, then to the farthest reaches of the sea!" His audience applauded, and some cheered. Diotrephes had our full attention. "If these bones were not entrusted to us, what more could I say? Shall we be like Smyrna? Or Pergamum?"

"Never!" cried a gravelly voice from the back. It sounded familiar but I couldn't place it.

"No—we are not like other cities!" Diotrephes affirmed. "And these bones, on this mountain, are the sign of a higher path!" It was almost too much. Gaius looked my way, and caught me rolling my eyes. He grimaced, and shook his head dolefully.

Just tell them the truth, Diotrephes. *Her bones have already left. They're resting peacefully in Jerusalem, where they belong.*

WEEK IV

I mentioned Xanthe yesterday, but it occurs to me I said nothing about her. We can't have that.

Xanthe is one of the Believers who loves Gaius' stories as much as I do. Now here's an interesting woman—she claims to be the last of the Amazon[24] warrior tribe that founded the city of Ephesus a thousand years ago. I don't know if it's true, but she believes it, and she certainly looks the part. She wears billowy, brightly-patterned trousers gathered at the ankle, and stands taller than most of the men. (She towers over me; I'm shorter than most of the women.) But her most interesting trait of all is the tattoos.

In Ephesus a tattoo is a sign of slavery. The city is packed with slaves, and each of them has some kind of mark—some on their hand, some on their forehead, and a few in other places. Even the freedmen have the marks, because there's no way to erase them.

Xanthe's tattoos, however, aren't symbols of subjugation, but rather identity and pride. On the left side of her neck is a crossbow paired with a battle axe. She tells me she received it at her coming of age. On the right side of her neck is a staurogram[25]—a sign of her newfound faith in Messiah. I can't imagine who agreed to give it to her; I don't know any Believers who possess that skill. But the symmetry between the two marks is stunning. Inspiring, even. Since Xanthe joined us three years ago she's sat and learned at my feet almost every day. The Jerusalem trip was the longest we've been apart since then. I missed her—she asks the best questions.

---

[24] Although the legend of the Amazons is a matter of some dispute, Greek historians such as Herodotus and Strabo attest to the historical existence of this band of female warriors in Asia Minor.

[25] A staurogram (⳨), also known as a *tau-rho,* or a monogrammatic cross, is a symbol that combines the Greek letters *tau* (T) and *rho* (P). It is one of the earliest Christian symbols, designed to visually represent Jesus on the Cross.

Omer 23 | Monday

As I think about the Hebrew believers in Rome, my thoughts start to spin relentlessly in my head. The issues with my old church are legion, but not one of them is new to me. When trouble comes, and sooner or later it does, we all tend to look for the exit. And those who exit the faith usually go out the same door they came in. I'm reminded of Jesus' parable of the sower—every belief background provides a unique soil for the weeds and thistles of falsehood to spring up. When trouble comes, it's painfully easy to predict which lies will resurface.

So as shocking as their circumstances might be, they are almost inevitable. Many of the problems Junia described arise from the Essene mindset, and as such, they rear their heads in Ephesus as much as they do in Rome. Actually it's a bigger problem here, because there are ten times as many (former) Essenes here.

I've known this mindset from an early age—my uncle Mordecai was a devoted Essene, in the Capernaum house. He never missed an opportunity to fill my head with ideas from Qumran[26], much to the consternation of my Abba. *Oh, the arguments they had.*

I've dealt with angel worshipers, incarnation skeptics, virgin-birth deniers, circumsizers, and proponents of "total grace"—and I have a box full of teachings to prove it. But sorting through it all, and figuring out how to cut through the noise and speak to the heart of this wounded community? That's going to take a lot of prayer.

Omer 24 | Tuesday

Gaius paid us a visit this morning to make plans for this year's Second Passover, which is just six days away.

---

[26] Qumran was the base of operations for the Jewish sect called the Essenes.

Like last year, he'll be leading the liturgy, and he came to ask us for help running the meal. Moses instituted the Second Passover thirty days after the first one, for anyone who found themselves ritually impure, or away on a journey the first time around. [27]

Gaius will lead it just like he did a month ago, and I assume Diotrephes will assist him. Aquila and I will do the readings and help the servers. I always love the Second Passover. It's so intimate—There are rarely more than forty or fifty participants. The first one has hundreds.

Lately I've seen more and more Gentiles show up to celebrate Passover. I always wonder how much of the Hebrew they understand. (Should we be offering a separate Seder in Greek? Before James' decision at the Council twelve years ago, this would have been unthinkable.) [28] It's also interesting how Believers have turned Passover into such a community event. Unbelieving Jewish families, by contrast, usually just celebrate it at home.

Omer 25 | Wednesday

I was browsing casually in the Agora this afternoon, looking at fabric samples, when my body suddenly crumpled and hit the ground. *Am I having a seizure?* I wondered in a panic. I shook my head and looked around to see plums and pomegranates rolling by. Some booths had collapsed, and people were shouting anxiously back and forth. *Definitely not a seizure. An earthquake?*

Just then I felt a hand on my shoulder, and heard a familiar husky voice again. "My darling Priscilla! Are you quite alright?" I spun around,

---

[27] Numbers 9:9-13

[28] Exodus 12:43-45 limits participation in the Passover Seder to the circumcised. However, Acts 15:1-31 describes the Council of Jerusalem in AD 50, wherein Peter argued, and James decided, that Gentiles should not be required to become circumcised converts to Judaism in order to join the Church, or participate in activities such as a Passover Seder.

a bit off my guard.

"Nicolas! Deacon Nicolas."

"Present and present." He grinned a little too widely, and reached out help me to my feet. I stood up, quickly dusting off my robe. I looked around to see people frantically gathering their wares and restoring their displays.

No one appeared to be hurt, so I helped the fabric dealer re-fold his disheveled inventory. Nicolas waffled for a moment, then picked up a stray belt of undyed canvas and rolled it up again. He handed it back to the merchant without looking at him.

"So that was an earthquake?" I asked him, breathlessly. "I've never felt one before. Not since our Messiah was crucified, anyway."

"It was indeed. I've experienced a few myself, some much stronger than this. What you just witnessed was either a weak tremor, or a strong one far away." I nodded slowly, wondering if somewhere else a city now lay in ruins.

"So what were you seeking here at the Agora?" he asked, changing the subject.

"Oh nothing, just some fabric for Seder tablecloths. The Second Passover is just a few days away, you know. Will you be joining us?" I asked him. He recoiled slightly, then covered his mouth with his right hand as if to stifle a guffaw.

"No, my dear Priscilla. I will not be there." He collected himself, and paused to weigh his options. "It surprises me a bit that you see any value in that. But if this is how you exercise your freedom, who am I to disparage it?"

He started to leave, but turned back to give a slight bow in my direction. "Until next time, my dear!"

Omer 26 | Thursday

Nicolas' words yesterday kept ringing in my ears as I made my selections at the market, as I walked home, as I ate dinner, and as I tried to sleep. "If this is how you exercise your freedom…" What does my freedom have to do with it? I would have asked him, but he always ends our conversations as quickly—and quixotically—as they begin.

And yet, he seems to enjoy talking to others at great length. Today I had more business to do in the Agora, and saw him again, seated in the fruit market talking passionately to Diotrephes. And when I left the market two hours later they were still there.

I can't help but wonder what they were talking about. I've never seen Diotrephes look so happy.

Omer 27 | Friday

The Second Passover is in three days, and Gaius has taken ill. I wish there were a silver lining to this, but I can't see one. His daughter Isadora who lives with him said he woke up groaning and weeping just before dawn. She summoned their doctor right away, and John, Aquila and me just after that.

By the second hour all the church leaders in Ephesus were at his house, and many church members as well. (John couldn't be here until evening—he and Milos spent the last few days in Miletus, and were traveling back today.)

All we did was pray for hours. The walls are now soaked with intercession, both inside and out. This is the legacy of a ministry of wisdom and kindness—one which we hope is far from over. Blessed are you, ADONAI our God, King of the universe, and Messiah of the nations. You take up our pain, you bear our suffering, and by your stripes we are healed!

I don't know what the doctor did, but at least Gaius is sleeping now. He looks awful—pale, panting and soaked in sweat. His hands clench and unclench even in his sleep. Isadora is panicked—right now she's fretting over whether to change out his wet bedclothes, for fear of waking him.

An hour after the doctor left, we felt another tremor. A few scrolls rolled off the shelf, and one of Gaius' medicine bottles fell and shattered on the floor. I heard some locals arguing over whether it was an "aftershock" (whatever that means) or a different event altogether. Whatever it was, it didn't wake Gaius, so Isadora decided it was safe to go ahead and change him into something dry. Whatever the doctor gave him was no weak potion.

Awhile later, when it looked like some of Gaius' visitors might be turning to go about their day, Diotrephes stepped onto a chair and called the house to attention. "Today we cry out to Almighty God," he declared, "through Christ Jesus and in the Spirit, to descend upon his servant Gaius with healing in his wings." At first I couldn't tell if he was preaching or praying.

"God, you have promised through your Son, that where two or more are gathered in your name, there you are with them. At this moment forty-seven of us are gathered in your name to rebuke the powers of darkness. And the prayers of the righteous profit much! Grant us this request in your Spirit today, and bring health and wholeness to your servant Gaius!" A chorus of *amens* filtered through the house, but I squirmed a little. This is a common reaction of mine whenever Diotrephes speaks, but I try not to let it show.

The prayer continued, but with a shift in tone. "And yet," Diotrephes paused interminably, praying in tongues under his breath. He squeezed his eyes shut, as if to hold tears at bay. His voice returned, trapped inside his throat. "And yet, not as we will, but your will be done, O Father. If the spirit of Gaius should depart from his body today, make us strong for the battle ahead…"

Battle? What battle?

"…and endow those leaders with power and strength who rise up in his place. And the body of the Lord say, *Amen."*

The body of the LORD said "Amen," but with less confidence than before. What does one make of a prayer like that? Is Diotrephes praying back the powers of darkness, or giving up without a fight? I hope it's the former—we can't afford to lose Gaius now.

Omer 28 | Saturday

Once John arrived last night, he and Apollos stayed by Gaius' side around the clock. Milos has served as their runner, going back and forth to the Agora for food, medicine and anything that might keep Gaius comfortable. Hundreds of red spots had now appeared on his face, hands and presumably the rest of his body. His fever rages on, and he can't keep anything down except water.

Some are calling it smallpox. I pray desperately that they're wrong, but I fear that they're right. Demetrius, Thea, Xanthe, Aquila and I have vowed to Isadora to visit him twice a day, every day until he's recovered. His sitting room has been converted to a night-and-day prayer vigil, as Ephesian Believers filter in and out.

Once this morning my grief and stress was steadied by that anchor of hope, as I considered the stories of all the individuals gathering for prayer in that room. There's Spiros, who was freed from slavery at age seventy. There's Basil, who lost his entire family, and almost his life, when his house collapsed. There's Helena, who has four children, and took in seven of her brother's after he died. There's Tassos and Lyra, who aren't even Believers, but Gaius buys all his clothing from them in the market.

Every hour or so, Apollos comes downstairs to greet the visitors, and provide an update on Gaius. When the news is especially troubling, he adds a special memory about our brother, being careful to speak of him in the present tense. To hear Apollos tell it, the love and compassion of Gaius is second only to that of Jesus himself. And when Apollos tells it, no one doubts it.

Seeing Basil, Spiros, Helena, Tassos, Lyra and so many others, from so many countries and so many languages praying together gives me goosebumps. Better than that, it gives me flashbacks to that Sunday almost thirty-two years ago, when we found ourselves at the Temple surrounded by people from every corner of the world.

None of us disciples were travelers, or worldly wise at the time. We all spoke Hebrew and Aramaic, and some spoke a smattering of Greek. So as more and more Jews poured in from the diaspora to celebrate Shavu'ot [29] at the Temple, we felt increasingly provincial. But every time someone talked about the command to make disciples in "Jerusalem, Judea, Samaria and the ends of the earth," [30] someone else would remind us that Jesus simply said to "wait." So that's what we did. We gathered in an upper room to pray, and at the Temple to celebrate. In our eyes the world had been turned upside-down, but we just continued on like everything was normal. The Twelve. The Seventy. James and his brothers. Aquila. Mary and the women. All of us.

We may have had no plan, but that didn't mean we had no clue. "Stay in the City—" Jesus said on Omer 40, before his ascension. That's easy. No one *left* Jerusalem during the final week of the Counting of the Omer. If you were still there from Passover, it's because you were staying for Shavu'ot, "—until you are clothed with power from on high." Something was going to happen on the day of Shavu'ot. We couldn't plan it. All we could do was wait.

---

[29] Shavu'ot is the Jewish Feast of Weeks
[30] Matthew 28:16-20, Acts 1:8

When the morning arrived, we were all in our usual place at the Temple. At the third hour, the *shofar*[31] blast came, and the account of Moses at Mount Sinai was read aloud:

Then Moses went down from the mountain to the people, consecrated them, and then, they washed their clothing.

In the morning of the third day, there was thundering and lightning, a thick cloud on the mountain, and the blast of an exceedingly loud shofar. All the people in the camp trembled.

Then Moses brought the people out of the camp to meet God, and they stood at the lowest part of the mountain. Now the entire Mount Sinai was in smoke, because ADONAI had descended upon it in fire. The smoke ascended like the smoke of a furnace. The whole mountain quaked greatly.

When the sound of the shofar grew louder and louder, Moses spoke, and God answered him with a thunderous sound.

Then ADONAI came down onto Mount Sinai, to the top of the mountain. ADONAI called Moses to the top of the mountain, so Moses went up.[32]

Purified garments. Fire and smoke. A thunderous sound from heaven. We listened to the Scriptures, and in that moment we knew we were about to be "clothed in power from on high," but we were terrified to imagine what it might mean.

That was when the wind came. Not from the East or the West, but straight down on our heads from above.[33] One hundred thousand hands went up to shield our heads from the onslaught, but it was no use. The wind forced everyone to the ground. We feared the entire city would

---

[31] Shofar: Trumpet fashioned from a ram's horn
[32] Exodus 19:14-20
[33] The account of the outpouring in Acts describes "the sound of a violent rushing wind." It is presumed here that this was not simply a sound, but refers to an actual wind event. The direction of the wind—from above—is speculative.

collapse under the pressure. But then it stopped in an instant, and I felt a burning sensation in my hands, as if my hair had caught fire. And yet, there was no pain. I jerked my hands away from my head in surprise, and looked at my companions, who all had flames on their heads as well. *What is going on?* I wondered incredulously.

I quickly found Aquila, and warned him that his hair was on fire. But my words sounded strange, as if I were speaking Egyptian. Aquila shook his head in confusion, and replied in something like Akkadian. *Was this the Tower of Babel all over again?* Just as I was about to panic, my heart felt a rush like my chest was going to explode, and that's when the strange-sounding words came pouring out of my mouth—not one at a time, but all in a row like water gushing from a rock. My hands floated into the air, and I made one declaration after another in random syllables; in an unknown tongue.

I learned afterward that some passersby were accusing of us of drinking too much wine. I felt honored to join my hero Hannah, mother of Samuel, in that accusation. Drunkenness without wine is a sure sign of true spiritual abandon before God. [34] No, we were not drunk, but perhaps we were insane. In that moment, I felt like I truly had lost my mind. But my spirit reassured me that it would return soon enough, and the syllables kept coming.

Suddenly I knew: My words were a prophecy. They were gospel. I didn't know what I was saying, but I nevertheless felt truth coursing through my veins, and warming my bones. I saw the faces of my brothers and sisters doing the same. I saw foreigners all around us with gaping eyes and slackened jaws.

We'd all come to celebrate the arrival of the Children of Israel at a Holy Mountain. The receiving of a Law. The birth of a Nation. But now a new Word was being spoken: the new Holy Mountain was the *Temple.* And the new Temple was *us.* The Law that was once etched on stone was

---

[34] 1 Samuel 2:5

now being written on our hearts. The Nation once birthed now had a message for *every nation,* spoken in *every language,* and delivered with a mighty wind and a fire from heaven.

Where once ADONAI clothed his chosen leader with radiant power, he was now placing his mantle of authority on all who believed in the Son. And in that moment we were truly clothed with power to be his witnesses in Jerusalem, but also in Judea, Samaria and the ends of the earth.

Shavu'ot would never be the same again. And neither would anything else.

WEEK V

I'm sitting here again, in Gaius' house. Praying alone, praying with Apollos, praying with visitors, and writing. My sinuses are congested and I have a headache. I've been assured that it's just a cold, not smallpox, so I'm going to drink more water than usual, and try to keep working. Aquila agreed to bring my writing table so I can work from here when I'm not praying or conversing. Obviously at the moment I'm writing *this*, but I've also been translating James, and writing my letter to the Hebrew Believers in Rome. There's so much I want to say; I don't know how to keep it brief.

It's afternoon now, and in this moment I'm just thankful that Gaius is finally sleeping. Bless ADONAI, he's less sweaty and agitated than before, but his fever is still raging, and there are no signs of recovery. Diotrephes has been in and out a lot—he seems very focused on preparing for the Second Passover tomorrow. I don't blame him. Even though it's a small gathering, this is his first citywide event to lead. (To be honest, I'm not sure if his Hebrew is up to it. He was raised by a Jewish mother and a Greek father.) Every now and then Gaius is coherent enough to give him some advice, but failing that he'll ask John or Aquila. Not me, though. I don't think Diotrephes has ever intentionally talked to me.

Aquila ate lunch here with me, along with Apollos, John and Milos. After that, Aquila went home, and John and Milos went back upstairs, so Apollos and I sat and talked for a while. I noticed that the braided candles we lit last night were still sitting out on the table, so I began to put them away.

"Did you light the *Havdalah* candles growing up?" I asked Apollos.

"My mother did. Father never showed an interest."

"Do you know that was my favorite time of week? To this day, I'm always glad when the Sabbath is over. That's quite a thing for a rabbi's daughter to say isn't it?" I confessed. Apollos just smiled.

"It's difficult for me to relax," I said. Apollos laughed as if he didn't believe me. "Just ask Aquila! He has no trouble at all. He'll just find a place to recline and pray, or watch the clouds, but I always want to fill the time. I like to move. I like to work." I held up my hands to show him the ink stains, like a leper's spots—marks of my fallen nature. "I suppose Jesus has freed us from the Sabbath mandate, so it's not a sin, but I keep remembering the look on Abba's face whenever my sisters and I tried to do too much on the Sabbath. Unless it was to serve him extra challah."

That's when Apollos put his finger to his chin, and spoke up. "Don't you know that the creation of ADONAI never ceases?"

"What do you mean? It says very clearly, 'and on the seventh day God rested.'"

"God *caused* all things to rest. In his fruitfulness, God *created* Sabbath. Not passively but actively. Just as the property of fire is to burn, it is the property of God to be always creating." Apollos' eyes twinkled, and his voice grew in intensity without losing its suppleness. "Do not think of Sabbath as an absence, but as a presence. Not as idleness, but as fruitfulness. Remember Pharaoh?"

"I'm not *that* old, Apollos!"

He grinned. "Pharaoh tried to defeat Sabbath, because the Hebrews were too numerous. Too fruitful. Even a wicked emperor can see that the Sabbath and Fruitfulness are forever linked."[35] His gestures caused his words to bloom in front of him like a rose, and his eyes grew brighter. "If we can learn from Pharaoh, the enemy of Sabbath, how much more from Jesus, the Lord of the Sabbath? When we abide in Jesus, do we not enter into the rest of God? For six days we have life—new life, real life. And on the seventh day we have life *to the very fullest!* Life we do not have to leave behind at *Havdalah*. Do not stop for the Sabbath, Priscilla. Press on in Jesus to *create rest* that refreshes the body and mind, to *produce fruit*

---

[35] As a renowned teacher from the city of Alexandria, it is presumed that Apollos was a student of Philo of Alexandria, sometimes referred to as the "first theologian." This exhortation on Sabbath rest is drawn directly from a teaching of Philo (Special Laws II).

that feeds the spirit."

"Bless ADONAI," I said, hiding my grin. "The student becomes the teacher."

"You always say that."

My heart is heavy for my old church in Rome. While they watch and pray for angels to swoop in and rescue them from trouble, they neglect the stranger—the foreigner and the pagan—and in doing so have dismissed their angels unaware.

I was spurred to this thought by Aquila's teaching this morning from the Torah portion, where Leviticus restates the Ten Commandments, then goes further. He showed us how it contained the seed of Jesus' greatest teaching: to love ADONAI, and to love our neighbors as ourselves. "We are not all scholars like Priscilla," he said, just as I was blowing my nose, "but Jesus shows us that we can all handle Scripture.

"If you read a word that perplexes you, just ask, 'How does this teach me to love God with my heart, soul and mind? How does it teach me to love my neighbor?' When Jesus said that the Law and Prophets hang on these two things, he gave us the keys to all of Scripture. Not everyone will be able to open every lock. But no one is left outside."

I'm anxious about the Seder this evening. Gaius is feeling no better, and I worry that his illness will cast a pall on the festivities. *ADONAI, let your hand of blessing and oil of anointing be on the head of Diotrephes tonight.* I sighed. *Don't let him ruin my favorite thing.*

Omer 30 | Monday

I'm feeling a little better now, though sometimes I have to stop writing for a minute when my eyes start to jitter. It's the morning after the Second Seder, and I have to be honest—I'm a little shocked.

Diotrephes pulled it off. His Hebrew was far more refined than I imagined, and he glided effortlessly through the fifteen steps. The gathering was also better attended than ever.

Still, some of his commentary raised the hairs on my neck. I can't put my finger on it, but he sounds different than I've ever heard him before. It's nothing overtly false or misleading—but the spirit of his message is wrong. I wish I'd written it down, but I spent most of the evening with a jar of wine in my hands, refilling the cups. Here's a little of what I can remember:

"Passover is called the Feast of Freedom since it memorializes the night when the faithful were protected by the blood of the lamb. Tonight, we Believers memorialize the blood of a different lamb: Jesus, the Lamb of God. And we celebrate a different freedom—not from slavery, but from the chains of moral law."

Why did he promise freedom from *the chains of moral law?* Why not just say freedom from *sin?* And for Freedom he used the word *chofesh,* which implies personal license, instead of *cherut,* which is the power to do right. My students mix those up all the time—was he just confused?

One more. "Each person in every generation must regard himself as having been personally set free from Egypt," he declared. "What is your Egypt? Are you bound to money? To power? To religion? To marriage? The Lamb has come to break your chains and loose your bonds, for if the Son has set you free, you are free indeed."

Freedom again. The message isn't wrong, but I couldn't let go of the words *religion* and *marriage.* Naturally, it's possible to make an idol out of anything, including religion and marriage. But I couldn't shake the sense that he was taking it further than that. Have we not committed ourselves to our spiritual brothers and sisters? Have we not willingly bound ourselves in marriage? Should marriage not be kept pure as a picture of Messiah and the Church?

More questions than answers. The odd thing is, I like questions. I just don't like *these* questions. Something is wrong.

I have a spot, in the hills above the harbor, that no one knows about. In a chaotic city like this, sometimes the only option is to retreat to the high places like Jesus did, to think and pray and watch the ships.

Religion and marriage. What two words define my life more than those? I am a religious teacher. I am a wife. I used to be a tentmaker, but not as much anymore. I am a daughter and a sister, an aunt and a cousin, but I live so far from the people who call me those things.

Religion and marriage. Are these idols to me? If ADONAI abandoned us—if the Spirit departed from us, heaven forbid—could I just continue on as always? Would I teach my lessons and pray my prayers all the same? If my marriage became void of all meaning, would I continue to live, and eat and sleep with my husband? If so, are these not signs of idolatry? Of empty devotion?

I've never liked Diotrephes, and I don't think he likes me. But that doesn't make him wrong. If the Spirit of God has indeed written the Law on our hearts, why shouldn't my own heart be my guide? Am I listening carefully to my heart, as Diotrephes would say?

On the other hand, some acts really do lead to death, no matter what my heart tells me. Some choices are dangerous, and some are just plain wrong. So, what if my heart can *deceive me?* As a teacher I claim to be mature. I don't subsist on spiritual milk anymore, but meat. I should be able to discern good from evil, light from dark. I know better than to engage in behavior that profanes the blood of the covenant—that tramples on the Son of God, and insults the Spirit of God! [36]

Is this what Diotrephes wants? I hope not. He's my brother in the Messiah, so I need to give him the benefit out the doubt. Surely he just wants the body to experience the kind of freedom Jesus won for us at the Cross. After all, if the Son has set us free, we are free indeed!

---

[36] See Hebrews 10:29

When I looked up from my writing just now, I noticed a ship floating into the harbor with an Achaean flag. The ship itself was unremarkable, but it occurred to me that it was the third ship from Achaea in the last hour. Not to mention three ships from Macedonia, and two more from Italy. They have nowhere to dock—it's been a busy morning, apparently.

I put away my spiritual struggle for a moment to count the ships— twenty-nine! I've never seen so many at once. I also see countless small oared vessels trying to fill in the cracks between merchant ships.

I couldn't ignore the sense that something strange was going on in the harbor, so I left my solitary place and hiked down the hill to the docks. When I arrived, I was swarmed by bandaged and bleary-eyed travelers moving in every possible direction to collect their possessions and figure out what to do next. An open ear to their conversations was all I needed to conclude that these people were refugees—fleeing trouble in their homelands, against all hope, starving and looking desperately for a place to survive.

What on God's good earth would cause them all to arrive at once?

Omer 32 | Wednesday

Early this morning, John called on Aquila and me to talk about the influx of migrants. They weren't just coming from the sea, they were flowing in by foot from the Asian inland—mostly from the region of Phrygia.

"Surely you remember those earthquakes we've felt over the last two weeks," Aquila said. I nodded slowly, and felt my heart beginning to seize up within me. "The first one was a massive quake throughout Macedonia and Achaea. Hundreds of cities are damaged."

I clapped my hand over my mouth. "What about—"

"Yes," John anticipated. "The church at Corinth. And Athens. And Thessalonica, Philippi, and Berea. But it gets worse." I took a deep breath

75

and Aquila resumed the news.

"The second tremor came from east of here, in Phrygia. Laodicea, Colossae, Hierapolis—Colossae is completely gone. There's nothing left. Monstrous tidal waves have even destroyed much of Cyprus. It's just— It's absolutely beyond comprehension."

"And, many—" my voice failed me for a moment. "Many are dead?"

"Yes, Priscilla. Many thousands." John choked. "People from every walk of life, perished in flame, or buried in rubble. Blessed are you, ADONAI our God, the true judge." John uttered the Hebrew mourning prayer as a reflex. I noted how jarring the word *judge* sounded to me in that moment. Those refugees did nothing to deserve this! And yet, I couldn't deny the truth of it—our God never leaves his judgment seat. Sometimes in the face of disaster all we can do is breathe out, breathe in, and whisper our hallelujahs through gritted teeth.

After his prayer the three of us sat in the dark without speaking for a long moment, and then another. We wept bitterly and imagined our dear friends in Corinth, dead, dying, fleeing or grieving. Perhaps even starving. We imagined all our brothers and sisters in Macedonia, in Achaea, in Phrygia—even those we'd never met. Even now the suffering exceeds all my ability to describe it.

After an hour, or perhaps three, Aquila dried his face and spoke. "These refugees, they look injured and hungry. Nothing to eat, nowhere to sleep. They have *nothing left*, John."

"I'm told that many cities are intact enough to support the victims, to bury the dead and feed the rest. But some are simply destitute. Their storehouses have collapsed, and wildfires have licked them clean. The survivors had no choice but to flee, and look for shelter and food somewhere else. Some came by ship across the sea, and others—like the Colossians—walked down the valley or found a rowboat to carry them to Miletus, and then, as we've seen, to Ephesus."

"How does God allow it?" I begged, still weeping.

"I don't know, Priscilla!" John nearly shouted at me, knocking me back. "Forgive me for thinking the kingdom was near! Forgive me for imagining our Messiah waiting in the wings to redeem the world to himself. Paul, for one, was nearly killed five times establishing the churches in those regions, and now—" John stood up and almost walked out, then turned around. He shook his head and breathed heavily for a moment, then sat back down.

"No, no, no—this isn't right. The answer is, my dear lady, that I don't know. I have no idea how God would allow this, or so many other tragedies. But one thing we can be quite certain of—this is not a judgment. Pagans, Jews and Believers alike have been lost their homes, their loved ones, or their lives. Every kind of city and town and homestead is affected, and we can see that in the faces, and hear it in the voices of these migrants all around us. Whatever their story, whatever their language or faith or point of origin, they have one thing in common—these people need *help.*"

"OK, they need help." Aquila said, sighing forcefully through his teeth. Overwhelmed but resolute. "What should we do?"

Omer 33 | Thursday

I found myself back at my spot above the harbor, thinking and praying. I sat on my rock and cried as I held the pain of the world for a moment. The sunlight glimmered off the waters and a salty breeze touched my face with a bittersweet kiss. In that moment I sensed a connection with something greater and lovelier.

I filled my lungs with air, wiped a final tear from my eyes, and stood up. The world is such a broken place. It was time to get back to work— and fix it, God help us.

I went back to Gaius' house, to check on him before I did anything else. I'm afraid he's getting much less attention than before. Diotrephes spent the day with the Ephesian Council, petitioning them to send the migrants home. A handful of church members have joined his effort, but they are in the minority. By and large, the Believers in Ephesus have rallied like never before to help the migrants.

John is tending to their spiritual needs, and has appointed Demetrius to coordinate the city-wide church to provide them with food, clothing and somewhere to sleep. I've never seen anything like it. Every house church, and many houses that aren't churches, are filled to the brim with migrant men, women and children, sleeping on the floor. Food is being donated by the wagonload—bread, olives, dates, and fish—to keep body and soul together.

At first, we took in four families and a pair of individuals. But then about dinnertime, Demetrius arrived at our house with a cart full of tent materials: linen and burlap, thread and rope, needles and thimbles, knives and awls. He told us he'd found another home for our guests, because our house was needed as a tent factory.

"The volunteers are on their way. You'll need to teach them how to make tents. Quickly." He started thumbing through the cart of supplies. "Everything you need should be here—" Demetrius was a craftsman himself, so I trusted him to know. "—except for the ropes. There's barely enough in here for two tents. All the rope dealers in town are tapped out. I'll have to send someone to Miletus to check there."

"Oh!" I suddenly remembered. "Don't do that. I heard Nicolas of Pergamum is back in town. He sells ropes all over the Empire—all lengths and sizes, he says."

"Is that right?" Demetrius replied. "I've never heard of him. But if he's in town—"

"I'll pay him a visit in the morning," I offered, a bit too brightly. "We have to come through. We can't turn our backs on our city, can we?"

Aquila looked confused for a moment, but then he smiled. "Not for a moment. Go, my love. God will provide."

By the third hour this morning I was strolling purposefully down the Curetes, past the Agora, and up the slope into the hillside villas overlooking the harbor. I came to the house where I'd heard Nicolas was staying. The entrance featured a large double outer gate, made of solid oak inlaid with swooping patterns of exotic woods.

A stoic servant named Constantine opened the gate and we walked through a marble archway and into a lush and elaborate courtyard. The tranquil sounds of Asian songbirds and a babbling fountain filled the space, instantly releasing the built-up stress in my neck and shoulders. A strange voice in the back of my mind spoke to me. *I should come here more often.*

I arrived at the inner gate, monitored by an alert-looking young woman, who greeted us with a bow. "Welcome. My master calls me Zoe. How may I serve his guests today?"

"Hello, Zoe. I have come to visit your master, Deacon Nicolas," I announced. "He is not expecting me." Zoe bowed again, and ducked inside. I waited only a moment before encountering the smiling face of the man himself, opening the door.

"My dear Priscilla! What a delightful surprise! Welcome to my home-away-from home. Not quite as splendid as my estate in Pergamum, but serviceable, wouldn't you say?" He didn't wait for me to answer. "But where are my manners? Would you care for anything to eat or drink?"

"Oh, thank you but—"

"I know just the thing!" He double-stepped out of the room and returned quickly with a small ornate jug. "A special vintage from the hills near my estate."

Before I could decline again, he'd placed a full silver goblet in front of me, and poured another one for himself. Then he reclined across from me and took a sip. I took one as well.

"This is good," I said, relishing the understatement. In truth it was the best thing I'd ever tasted. I sipped gingerly from the goblet again, resisting the urge to tip it back.

"So!" Nicolas said. "To what do I owe the pleasure?"

"Yes, I've come to ask for a favor."

"Of course, my dear. You can have all the ropes you need."

"What? How did you—"

Nicolas laughed uproariously. "Oh, my friend! You do not know how often I'm asked this. And I knew the rope dealers in Ephesus were sold out, so what else could it be?" He sat up straight, then leaned in close to me. "I should tell you, though—I nearly always say no."

"I— I don't know what to say…"

"Your friendship is reward enough, my dear. To be known to a legendary teacher such as yourself—that is a true honor. I see I have embarrassed you, Priscilla, but there is no need! You have earned every drop of the esteem you receive, and so much more. I am truly inspired by what you've achieved as a woman, in a Church dominated by men."

I'd never heard anyone say this before. John always showed confidence in me, and Paul even affirms me in his letters from time to time. But nothing like this.

"Apollos once shared with me a teaching of yours. The Torah has a shadow of the good things to come—for this reason it can never, by means of the same sacrifices they offer constantly year after year, make perfect those who draw near. So when Messiah comes into the world, he says, 'Sacrifice and offering you did not desire—'"

"You talked to Apollos?"

"'—but a body you have prepared for me.'[37] By God's will we have been made holy through the offering of the body of Jesus once and for all. This is brilliant, Priscilla! It changed the way I think about sacrifice."

He quoted it perfectly. I could feel my cheeks getting flush. I swallowed my emotions and managed a gracious reply. "Thank you,

---

[37] See Hebrews 10:1-10

Nicolas. That's very kind of you to say."

"As I said, you deserve so much more than you receive." Nicolas squinted his eyes, rubbed his neatly-trimmed beard, and leaned into me. "Forgive my impertinence, Priscilla—" his husky voice had become smooth and intimate. "but I notice you have no children. Is this because of you? Or your husband?"

"Nicolas!" A bolt like lightning shot down my spine.

"I mean no offense," he countered defensively. "I will confess—I was not asking in good faith. In truth, I know the answer."

My anger quickly turned to vexation, and then confusion. I took a deep breath and sat up as tall as I could manage. "And?"

"It isn't you. How could it be? As I admitted, the question was an impertinent one. One for which you were not prepared, and for that you have my deepest apologies. I ask, only because you are a great, and accomplished, and *beautiful* woman, Priscilla. It would break my heart to know that you are receiving anything less than the most devoted admiration, in the marketplace, in the church, or in the home. The world is indeed a poorer place if you have fewer than *seven* children."

He called me *beautiful*. The last person who called me beautiful was Aquila. Ten years ago.

I don't remember what happened after that. I have some vague recollection of walking home with a contract in my hand, but I couldn't even say which road I took.

Omer 35 | Saturday

We spent the morning in the middle of a dozen belts of pale yellow linen, trying to observe the Sabbath by supervising today instead of sewing. Most of our volunteers are Gentiles, so they'll rest tomorrow while Aquila and I continue the work.

We're putting our complete trust in the Spirit to turn these novices into tradesmen in only a day or two. They're all learning so diligently. Even still, it's hard to imagine how we can make even a tiny dent in this gargantuan problem.

By mid-afternoon, I needed to step away. So many words kept swirling through my head. I needed to pray, to think, to breathe a little bit. So I walked out the door and headed for the northern gate and out of the city. Beyond the walls, I stepped off the Processional Way and onto a dusty farm road. For some reason I was imagining a walk along the still country lanes would do me good, but the countryside had changed. There was activity everywhere.

Ephesus was no stranger to crowds—while I'd been traveling, the festival to Artemis took place, as it does every year in the Spring. People come from all across the region, but it's organized. They bring their own tents. They bring money. And the merchants are ready, with shiploads of food, provisions and souvenirs to sell. A month later, everyone leaves.

I followed the road as it bent from north to east, and up a slope. When I rounded the top, I saw the sun rising behind the Artemision, casting its enormous shadow onto the vast plain below. And what I saw in that plain, stretching from horizon to horizon, stopped my heart.

Thousands upon thousands—*tens of thousands* of hopeless refugees scraping out a living. Some in tents, some in makeshift shelters, but most in nothing—exposed to the elements, just looking for a place to exist. *I had no idea.* Smoke from dozens of campfires curled to the sky. Screams from hundreds of babies reached my ears at once, alongside cries for help and shouts of desperation.

"No!" I wailed furiously at the camp. At heaven. At my own heart. *The gates of hell have no wrath like this!* My knees gave out, and I collapsed onto the road, sobbing in great waves, my chest heaving in pain.

ADONAI *have mercy on us!* I cried. *We are undone.*

WEEK VI

I had a nightmare last night—as I often do—that it was my turn to preach, but I hadn't spent a single minute preparing a message. I rose from my seat to speak to a full house but when I looked up it was just Nicolas of Pergamum. Flashing me that disarming smile. My eyes fluttered and I sat up in a cold sweat, then went downstairs to wash my face and get a drink of water. That was the moment I realized today was Sunday. And it was my turn to preach. And I hadn't prepared. My heart dropped into my gut.

The sun was already streaming in through the window, which meant our congregation would start showing up in less than an hour. Barely enough time to clean up, get dressed, and read once through today's portion.

It really was a full house, but no Nicolas. *Why would he miss this?* I asked myself. *Miss what?* I replied. *I don't even know what I'm going to say.* I realized I was acting insane. It was just a dream. *Get it together, Priscilla.*

My turn came to stand up, and I stumbled my way through the sermon. I don't even remember what I said. The portion was from Leviticus again—about the purity regulations of the priestly office. I think I rambled about the insufficiency of the sacrificial system, and probably said something about Melchizedek. I don't remember who was there, or the looks on their faces as I preached. I'm guessing it was a mix of boredom and confusion.

The whole time I was talking I had a completely different dialogue in my head, thinking about the dream. *Does Nicolas have a point about freedom? What would John say? Nicolas is shifty, but John has been wrong before.* We Jews have a saying: "Two rabbis, three opinions." This is what it feels like in my mind. Two sides battling back and forth, producing three—or six, or ten—different conclusions.

Somehow I managed to wrap up my sermon and sit back down,

trying not to make eye contact with anyone. When worship was over I went straight upstairs and back to sleep. Suddenly I'm feeling sick again.

Omer 37 | Monday

Materials and volunteers keep showing up at our door, so the tent-making continues unabated, from dawn to midnight. It's been good to focus on manual work, when I can. Lately my mind feels like an upturned patch of soil—a garden relentlessly assaulted by a sharp, swinging blade. It could be cultivation, or chaos. I want to talk to Aquila but I don't know what I can share.

It's midnight now. Aquila has instructed every volunteer to put down their needles and get all the rest they can. But obviously, I'm not resting. I'm writing.

Maybe I should go downstairs and make another tent—work with my hands. It's the only thing that quiets the voices in my head. The babies screaming for milk, the women sobbing in the gutter, the men loitering about, afraid for their lives and afraid to show it. I want them to have homes again, to have lives again. I want them to be fed, to be sheltered, to be healed. On a good day, I want them to be blessed.

But most days I just want them to leave.

It makes me sick to read the words I just wrote. *What kind of person am I?* As the wise men say, if you want to find out what something is made of, first you have to break it. Earlier this afternoon, this is exactly what happened to me. I was preparing the fruits and vegetables for dinner when Aquila walked in with some news.

"Priscilla, did you hear? Daphne had her baby. *Babies,* actually. Twin boys!" The volunteers looked up from their needles and cheered a hearty blend of *mazel tov's* and *opah's* to the happy couple. But I didn't look up at all—I kept chopping a pomegranate. Nobody noticed until the applause died down, but the chopping didn't.

"Priscilla. Priscilla!" Aquila put his hand on my chopping arm. "Didn't you hear? Apollos is—"

"Yes, more offspring! What will that make? Twelve now?"

"Uh—four, actually."

"Well, either way. Good for Daphne! A worthy wife indeed, filling her husband's quiver." *Chop! Chop! Chop!* I freed my arm from Aquila's grip, and the volunteers returned to their sewing, pretending not to hear.

"Is that what you think makes a worthy wife?"

"You're right!" I turned on him, his eyes wide with surprise. I realized I was gesturing at him with my knife and dropped it. The blade clattered to the floor, barely missing a hapless cat. The laugh brewing in Aquila's eyes made me even angrier. "You're right. It's no credit to Daphne! Apollos is the worthy one. What kind of God would deprive such a man of a house full of beautiful and brilliant progeny?" *It's happening again. I can't hold my tongue to save my life.* "That woman, on the other hand, she doesn't deserve a thing. But you know who does?" I demanded.

"Priscilla, perhaps we should—" Aquila motioned for the door.

"I do!" My entire body felt like it was engulfed in flames. "*I'm* the one with the prophecy from the Baptizer. *I'm* the one who left home again and again to follow you and Paul and any *man* who asked. So I'm certainly *not* the one who's holding us back!"

Now Aquila's nostrils were flaring. He planted his feet. "What is *that* supposed to mean?"

"Nothing, Aquila. It's my fault for thinking you might understand. I'm going to check on Gaius now." I turned to stomp out, but the door was jammed shut in the frame.

Aquila leapt over. "I can help," he said calmly, and yanked it open.

"Thanks!" I barked. Then I stepped out and slammed it shut. But instead of turning left to Gaius' house, I turned right and rounded the corner into the alleyway beside our house. I stood with my back against the wall for a moment to catch my breath, then slid down to the ground and wept into my hands. *I need sleep. That's all.*

I don't know if it was half an hour or an hour and a half later, but Aquila found me in the alleyway—just sitting there, all sobbed out. He didn't touch me. He didn't say a word. He just sat down next to me in the dirt. Together we watched the plain stone wall in front of us go from light to dark. Eventually I put my head in his lap, and fell asleep.

Omer 38 | Tuesday

We woke up in our own bed this morning. (No, we didn't sleep all night in the alley.) My first thought this morning was that I have to talk to Apollos. I have to know what Nicolas has been saying to him. But even if Apollos appeared right in front of me, I don't know if I could trust myself to say anything true.

I'm so confused. My mind feels like a dinghy caught in a sea squall. Every ounce of confidence I once had—about the church, about Scripture, about myself—has just gone up in smoke. I don't even recognize myself anymore. I look around at my life, and I see that it's based entirely upon things that happened twenty or thirty years ago. What happens if those things disappear? What do I have left to stand on? *Maybe it's time to rip that anchor off our front door.*

The refugee crisis isn't helping. I've been through disasters before; refugees are usually respectful of their hosts. But Ephesus is completely overrun. The camp outside the walls is bad enough, but now the chaos has spread all throughout the city. Every block of every street is choked with suffering people. They have no place to go, and we have no place to hide from the sounds of desperation—men in the Agora quarreling over a fig, women crying out for *anyone* to take them in. Children—oh, but the children. They are the only ones silent. No laughs, no shouts, no cries of hunger. They just glare at me as I pass. *It's not their fault,* I keep reminding myself. *It's no one's fault. It's just a thing that happened.* Hopefully if I can repeat it enough times I might start to believe it.

Every second household in Ephesus has taken a family in, but they keep quiet. Some of the guests have actually abandoned their hosts in favor of people needier than they, and end up gnawing on leather belts in a garbage heap. Scripture tells us of a place of ultimate suffering, where the fire never fades and the worm never dies—where there is weeping and gnashing of teeth. I have seen that place now, in the eyes of these people.

I live there.

Omer 39 | Wednesday

I woke up well before dawn this morning and couldn't fall back asleep. So I found a reed and ink jar, and lit a candle in a quiet corner. At the first hint of light, I left home and headed for the Agora. I strolled around the perimeter of the market in a trance, and watched as a few bleary-eyed merchants arrived to set up, bodyguards in tow.

I wanted to pray as I walked. I wanted to cry out for a solution, but couldn't recall a single prayer I'd ever known. *I look to the hills. Where does my help come from?* That's all I could remember. All the knowledge and learning in my head were being drowned out by the shouts and the cries emanating from those very hills.

I turned from the Agora onto the street that leads back to my house, and almost stepped on her. A little girl, dressed in rags, lying face-down in the gutter. Five, maybe six years old. I crouched down to look closer. When I pulled her curly brown hair away from her face, I gasped.

Dear God. She's dead.

My heart shuddered violently. I put my hand over my mouth but it couldn't prevent my stomach from emptying itself onto the cobblestones beside me. I wiped my face, mopped my forehead, and turned off my brain. *You've done enough,* I told it.

I stood up resolutely, walked two blocks back to my house, swiped a cut yellow cloth from the top of a stack, then marched straight back to the little girl. I slid a corner of the cloth under her face, and spread the rest across her back. Then I tucked her left side in, and rolled her emaciated frame to the right, so the cloth would cover her as she turned over. Then I tucked the other side in and heaved her into my arms. *She's so light! Mercy, she hasn't eaten in weeks.*

Back in our courtyard, I laid her gently on a stone bench, found a spade and started to dig. I pierced the ground again and again, with every strike cursing the God of this hellish world. The God of earthquakes. The God of crumbling homes. The God of starving children. The God that would let a woman bury a child, but never bear one.

I finished the pit, and went back to retrieve the body. I crouched at the edge and laid her in as carefully as I could, but I dropped her the last few inches, and she thumped at the bottom. A lock of curly brown hair escaped from the cloth, and I couldn't ignore it. It looked just like mine, but without the gray. I should have tucked it back in, but instead I grabbed a knife, cut it off, and stuffed it into my robe.

I stood up and looked at the hole, with the long yellow shape at the bottom. Not so different from a fresh bolt of fabric, except for the body of a child inside. A voice in the back of my head spoke. *You've done well. She is at peace; her worries are over.*

Then it spoke again. *If you dig the hole a little larger, you could join her.*

I don't know how long I stood and pondered the body of the girl at the bottom of the pit, but eventually John interrupted me.

"Priscilla!" he called out. "There you are, dear lady!" He jogged up to me, and stopped a moment to catch his breath. Then he saw what I'd been doing. "Oh my. Who is this?"

"I don't know. I found her in the gutter." I held up the lock of hair for some reason. John kneeled at the edge of the hole, and reached down to lift the tassel at a corner of his tunic to his lips. Then he davened back and forth, reciting the Mourner's Prayer in Hebrew.

"Did you touch her?"

"Just her hair."

"Here, let me help." He picked up another spade, and together we filled in the pit. Then John found a wooden garden stake. "Do you have something to write with? A reed or a brush?" I went inside to get my writing kit, and brought it to him. He dipped the reed in the inkwell, and held it to the stake. "What should we name her?"

"Avrah," I said without thinking.

"Are you sure?"

"Her name is Avrah." John wrote four Hebrew letters on the wood, blew on it, and shoved the stake in the ground at the edge of the pit. "Here lies Avrah, peace be upon her. Blessed are you, ADONAI our God, the true judge. Amen."

"Thank you, John." My head was finally starting to clear. "Why did you come?"

"I need you and Aquila to meet me at the Artemision at the fifth hour tomorrow. Bring everyone you can. It's a new work, Priscilla. A work of the Spirit."

Omer 40 | Thursday

Why do you gaze with envy, you mountain peaks, at the mountain God desired for his dwelling? Yes, ADONAI will dwell there forever!

You went up on high. You led captivity captive. You received gifts from humanity, even from the rebellious—so that God might dwell there. Blessed be ADONAI! Day by day he bears our burdens—the God of our salvation![38]

---

[38] Psalm 68:17, 19, 20 (Quoted in Ephesians 4)

Day 40. Ascension Day, when Jesus' feet left this earth. It was thirty-two years ago and it feels like no time has passed at all. In a normal year we would spend this day in worship—recounting our memories, making disciples, and watching the sky for Jesus' return. This year, however, Omer 40 looked a little different.

After a normal morning of sewing tents and coaching volunteers, Aquila stepped outside to look at the sundial. "It's the fourth hour, Priscilla. Are you ready to go?" I had no idea what John had in mind for us at the Artemision, but I couldn't shake the look of hope in his eyes yesterday. *A new work,* he said. But I was afraid to hope. It's safer to expect disaster.

After Aquila and I stepped onto the Curetes, he gave me a quizzical look, and reached out to touch the ends of my hair to the left of my chin. I thought he was going to tell me my hair had dried funny this morning, but instead he just smiled and kissed me.

We continued through the Magnesian Gate and turned north onto the Processional Way. That's where Demetrius caught up with us. As we looked toward the temple, our eyes were greeted with that horrific sight—the plain of ultimate suffering. My soul was exhausted by it. And yet, it occurred to me to take a fresh look at the tents dotting the encampment. There were more tents now than ever, and well over half were a familiar shade of yellow.

"Who else has been making yellow tents?" I asked Demetrius.

"No one else. All the yellow linen goes to your house." Aquila and I gasped together. We stopped in our tracks. I glanced down at my hands, rubbed the blisters and callouses pensively, then looked up again. *Incredible.*

"So many," Aquila said breathlessly. "There are so many." We had focused all our attention on producing the tents and sending them out the door, we'd forgotten to count them. So I counted them—318 in this area alone. [39] More than the two of us (three of us, if you include Paul) could make in a year.

"Are they any good?" I whispered anxiously.

"They are perfect," Demetrius replied. "Exactly what we needed."

We continued walking, with the city wall and Mount Pion looming on our left, partially obscuring the temple ahead, as well as its environs. But as we progressed, the entire scene came into view. For the second time, we were stopped cold. "What's going on?" I asked. A throng of refugees crowded the path leading to the front of the Artemision from the west, waiting for something. I imagined the Children of Israel, watching all night as the Red Sea slowly parted.

"Better to see for yourself," Demetrius grinned. Aquila looked at me, and I met his gaze—again, afraid to hope. As we approached the throng, John spotted us and jogged up to greet us.

"You're here! Come on." He put his hands on our backs and almost pushed us toward the great gate. When we got closer, we saw a half-dozen clerics and city officials gathered at the entrance. After scanning the crowd for a moment, a portly man—Aquila told me it was Marcus, the head of the Ephesian Council—took a large key and opened the massive iron doors. Instantly, the crowd began flooding into the cavernous colonnade of the great Temple of Artemis.

"This way," John said, leading us around to our right. "We can enter through the southern gate." I had never been inside before, and I assumed John hadn't either. But perhaps I was wrong. When we stepped inside, I swooned. The sheer scale was overwhelming enough, but the sight of what was happening inside almost knocked me flat.

Between every pair of mammoth columns (of which I've been told there are exactly one hundred) was a table, piled high with fruits and vegetables—olives, grapes, dates, figs, pomegranates, oranges and pears. There were nuts, raisins, and breads. There was dried fish, salted chicken

---

[39] Genesis 14:14

and cured beef. There were brushes, clothing, soap, even perfume.

Later, as I meandered through the tables, I also saw tools, writing utensils, parchment, and dolls and toys for children. Some tables had landowners sitting behind them, ready to hire day-laborers. It was simply astonishing. Historic. A count of the tables, an estimate of the average amount of goods on each, produced a figure I just had to say out loud.

"This must have cost *eight million* drachmas." I ventured.

"Unbelievable." Aquila whispered. "Just—" and he trailed off. Words had no place here. So I just looked and listened. As we made our way toward the front entrance, we saw the crowd filtering through the tables, coming in our direction.

I thought about every time I'd ever approached this structure, and witnessed the crowds gathered outside, waiting to get in. They come from the four winds with votive offerings, arms full—and sometimes carts full—of fruits, vegetables, nuts, clothes, tools, scrolls. Anything that represented a personal sacrifice to gain favor with the goddess. Or to thank her for favors past. That's the only reason this monstrosity exists. But now, after centuries of receiving such gifts, the temple is giving back.

What was once an affront to the Spirit of God has now become an instrument in his hands. People are arriving, not with full baskets and carts, but empty hands and empty stomachs, and "those who were starving are hungry no more." [40]

After walking along the southern colonnade, we came around to the front. "What's through there?" I asked John, pointing at a gigantic double door, ornamented with friezes of nude figures engaged in hunting and farming, trading and fighting.

"Through there is the inner chamber. That's where the statue of Artemis sits."

---

[40] 1 Samuel 2:5

"Are they letting people in?"

"Not yet." John stood a little taller and scanned the crowd, as if he was looking for someone. "There's room in the Colonnade alone to accommodate a vast crowd of guests—to meet their needs and provide some shelter from the elements. The interior space would be exceedingly helpful to people, but we don't want to push our luck."

"We?" I caught John's eyes before they darted away. I ducked around to force him to look at me again. "You had something to do with this, didn't you?"

"My dear lady," John said, with an expression that was at once impish and ageless. "The heart of humankind is made for compassion. Who stopped to help the beaten man? Not the religious practitioners, but the Samaritan—the heathen and the foreigner. Is it not written?" he asked with a wink, "When these, who do not have the Law, do by nature the things of the Law, they show that the work of the Law is written in their hearts." [41] *Behold the words of Paul, sounding an awful lot like Scripture.*

Tears filled my eyes, and Aquila's too. We looked back out across the throng, and watched and listened. The cries of desperation which had filled our minds for days and days were slowly supplanted by cries of delight, of thankfulness, of hope. Every tribe, every nation, every race, every tongue. Able-bodied and lame, young and old, male and female, Jewish, Christian and pagan. All rubbed elbows together in joy. Not a single word of strife or rivalry was heard—there was enough for all.

I turned my eyes heavenward and saw a single cloud in front of the sun; the edges on one side were shimmering like the rim of a golden cup. Was this finally the return of Jesus? Certainly not—this is the wrong temple, after all. But those unforgettable words rang in my ears again, spoken by the men in white on that fortieth day of the Counting of the Omer: "This Jesus, who was taken up from you into heaven, will come in the same way as you saw him go."

---

[41] Romans 2:14a, 15a

John saw the cloud, too. When I turned to look at him he was gazing through tears at the sky. I stared at him for a long time before I spoke.

"Is he coming back, John?"

He laughed with a mixture of surprise and frustration—a laugh I know all too well. Hope and pain and grief and wonder and emptiness and love all wrapped up in a muddy cloak, wrung out, uncoiled and clapped against the wind. We are stained but cleansed. Soaked through but dry as a bone. Wrinkled and stretched and weary, but still intact.

At length, John replied. "See how the farmer waits for the precious fruit of the earth, being patient for it until it receives the former and latter rain. You also be patient. Strengthen your hearts because the coming of the Lord is near."[42]

I sighed. *Oh, James. How we miss you.*

John took a long, slow breath and returned his gaze to the Temple scene. "Yes, Priscilla, he is coming back." Then he turned to look at me—to look through me—and his eyes were deeper than the ocean. "But tell me, dear lady. Did he ever really leave?"

Just then I felt a slight tug at the end of my belt, and looked down. A painfully slender girl about six years old, with olive skin and dark brown hair, was looking up at me with bright and moistened eyes.

"Hello," I said in Greek, bending slightly at the waist.

She turned to look up at her mother, who whispered something into her ear. *"Shlama,"* she said in her tiny voice, wishing me peace in Aramaic, followed by *"Tebu lek."* Thank you. I placed a hand on the girl's head, and said a short blessing in Aramaic over her, over her mother and her family. I reminded them that *God alone* provides for all our needs, according to his riches in glory. Mother and daughter smiled brightly, and continued on.

"Where do you suppose they're from?" I asked Aquila.

---

[42] James 5:7b-8. This verbiage is presumed to have been part of James' well-known teaching before appearing in the epistle of James.

"It's hard to say. Judging by the accent—Galilee, I suppose. They were probably already refugees before the quake."

"There's still a long road ahead for them, isn't there?"

"There is indeed. So much is in ruins." Aquila drew me into his arms and we gazed at the scene before us. I considered the evils of poverty, of war, of disaster. Then I considered the miracle of sustenance spread out before our eyes. The unfettered smiles. The arms filled with food, and faces filled with hope.

What the enemy has planned for evil, God has turned to good. Blessed be God's name, forever and ever. Amen.

Omer 41 | Friday

This morning I headed straight to Gaius' house to check on him. I wanted so desperately to tell him about yesterday's events, but he was fast asleep. It's hard to see fewer and fewer people paying visits, as his illness stretches on. The only thing worse than being deathly ill is being forgotten and alone. Gaius is both.

After praying for him again, I decided to sit down at my writing table downstairs, and get some work done. I really ought to have gone home to the tent factory. But I was also feeling an urgency for my Hebrew friends in Rome. So I grabbed a reed, a page of parchment and a bottle of ink, and started writing.

I knew I was tired—I barely slept last night after all the excitement— but it was worse than I thought, because I found myself crossing out every line I could think to write. So I gave up. I pulled out James' letter, to resume my translating work. But as soon as I touched it I felt overwhelmed with grief, so I put it away and got out Jude's letter instead. *That's better.*

It was a few weeks ago when I last worked on this. It's a short letter, but thick with history and cosmology. There's Sodom and Gomorrah, and Michael the Archangel fighting with Satan over the body of Moses. There's the way of Cain, the error of Balaam, and the rebellion of Korah. Jude doesn't pull his punches with those who "slander what they do not understand." Such picturesque language—he declares them waterless rain clouds and fruitless fruit trees. Fruitless even in autumn, when they should be heavy with fruit. "Doubly dead" he pronounces them. It was starting to feel awfully close to home—almost as if Jude has someone in mind that he refuses to name.

Apparently even the thrill of translating was not enough to keep me awake, and I felt myself nodding off again. Next thing I knew I was suddenly roused by a weak and raspy voice. "Priscilla."

It startled me so badly I almost fell off my chair. It occurred to me that there was a little drool on my cheek, so I wiped it off, and felt my face turn red hot. "Gaius!" I exclaimed. "What are you doing?" He was standing at the bottom of the stairs, looking like death. I rushed over to get him back up to his bed, but instead he stood still, and pointed across the room.

"Isn't that your writing table? From your house?"

"Yes. Why?" Gaius's eyes fluttered, so I put my arm around him, and convinced him to walk back upstairs. But he didn't want to lie down—he just sat on his bed. I fetched him some water and food. He ate and drank, but just barely. I prayed with him again, and he asked me to catch him up on the events of recent days. After giving him the facts, I started to let my feelings spill out.

"I'm so confused about Nicolas," I confessed, "and Diotrephes. This new message about freedom is so slippery. It sounds like truth. But it isn't. Or—it mostly isn't." *Here we go. I'm going to stress out his heart, and he's going to die right here in my lap.*

"You're overthinking it, Priscilla," he whispered. It's possible I was overthinking it. He stared at me with those weepy yellow eyes, until my own started to water. His flesh was profoundly weak, but I could see the Spirit bubbling up behind his sullen countenance. Just when I was starting to feel awkward sitting there in silence, he spoke again.

"Look at the fruit," he whispered.

"The fruit?" I asked.

"Yes. Our brother John once told me something beautiful." Gaius spoke slowly, each word bearing eternal weight. "In our sin we cannot discern what's true and what's false. But we can look at the fruit. The fruit of falsehood is darkness and death. But the fruit of truth is light and life."

"They are fruitless trees…" I whispered to myself, turning away. *Does Jude know something that I don't?* I looked at Gaius again, searching for answers. "So, what should I say?"

"Words of light, dear one. Words of life. *Your words* are your fruit." His eyes fluttered, so I helped him back into his bed.

"One more thing, Priscilla." His eyes were closed tight now. "Get your writing table out of here."

"What?"

"You don't live here. You live with Aquila." I was taken aback by the rebuke. But I'd swear a faint smile crossed his lips.

"If you insist." I pulled the covers up to his chin and tucked them around his ailing frame. "Sleep well, sweet Gaius. May the healing hand of ADONAI be upon you."

Omer 42 | Saturday

What is happening to us? Maybe we're growing weary in our well-doing. Maybe we're giving Nicolas too big a stage. But whatever it is, the Ephesians Church is splintering like a sapling in a hailstorm.

I thought the miracle at the Artemision would breathe some life into us again, and bind us together in the power of the Spirit. But now the Jewish houses are refusing to accept God's willingness to use a pagan temple. They've pulled out of all city-wide efforts. They no longer accept Gaius or Diotrephes as their leaders.

As a result, the Greek houses—at the urging of Diotrephes—are shunning Jewish believers, and preaching against Israel. Then there are the Jews who have renounced their heritage altogether, citing its "love of the Law," to join the Greeks. If that weren't enough, some Greek houses are breaking away in support of certain fathers and husbands who want the "freedom" to abandon their families, or bring a second wife into the household. *Freedom.* There's that word again.

The sounds of calamity in the streets that used to come from starving refugees are now coming from the brothers and sisters in the faith. Theft, deception and adultery have brought men to blows too many times in the last few days to count. It's even affected the volunteers in our house, many of whom are too confused to know where they stand anymore. Our tent production is dwindling, and morale is dropping too.

Our own house church appears to be the only one left with both Jews and Gentiles. John told me yesterday that he was planning to join us tomorrow morning—I don't think he can tolerate his own spiritual family in its current state.

Reading back over this, it's like the letter from Junia is playing out in front of our eyes. Ephesus is turning into Rome, and it's happening fast.

ADONAI have mercy, I need to work on my letter. Give me the words. Bear the fruit of your Kingdom in me. And do it quickly.

WEEK VII

Omer 43 | Sunday

"Today is forty-three days, which is six weeks and one day of the Counting of the Omer. God has ordered our world to proclaim his message. From the movements of the stars, to the crawling ants beneath our feet, the Word of salvation is woven into the cosmos." Aquila preached from this week's portion in Leviticus. His voice was strained, tight with emotion. My head was still spinning from last week's drama, but as my husband spoke of the order of creation, I felt my soul being soothed. Quieted. Beckoned.

"Six days you shall work, but on the seventh day you shall rest. That is the Sabbath Day, completing one week.

"Seven weeks you shall count from the Passover, and on the fiftieth day you shall celebrate the spring harvest. That is Pentecost.

"Six years you shall sow your fields, prune your vineyards and gather your crops, but in the seventh year the land shall rest. That is the Sabbath Year."

"Seven Sabbath Years you shall count, and in the seventh month of the fiftieth year you shall sound the trumpet to proclaim a year of freedom. That is the Jubilee Year. In those days we celebrate a harvest, not of barley or of wheat, but of souls. As our Messiah said in the synagogue to inaugurate his ministry, 'The Spirit of ADONAI has sent me—to proclaim freedom to the prisoner!'"

The congregation erupted in shouts and hallelujahs, clapping their hands and singing their praises to the God as if each of us had just been freed from captivity ourselves in that moment. And those whom the Son sets free are free indeed—not from religion or from marriage, but from sin and death. This is it—this is the Fruit! Love, joy, peace, patience and all the rest. Religion and marriage are not a prison cell holding us back, but two of the many ways in which we produce and share this fruit.

As I looked around it occurred to me that we've never had this many at our house before. Even for Passover. Nearly half of them appeared to be refugees, but one face stood out to me. It was one of the men who opened the temple to the crowd, three days ago. *That's right, it's Marcus. The head of the Ephesian council!* He looks different when he's not in charge. Shorter, perhaps.

Aquila fed off the fervent energy of the assembly, as he preached mightily about freedom. Freedom from captivity, freedom from oppression, freedom from sin. But more important than our freedom *from,* he explained, was our freedom *to.* Freedom to worship. Freedom to follow. Freedom to love our neighbors as ourselves. Our neighbors. I scanned the room and caught looks of gratitude and wonder, looks of guilt and exhaustion, looks of resolution and grit. Every man, woman and child had a different reaction to that word—neighbors—and what it means to love them. Or to be loved by them.

Aquila finished on a high note, and a time of boisterous worship followed. Brothers and sisters cried out to God together in thankfulness and petition, in repentance and forgiveness. Words of hope were shared with the hopeless, and hands of healing were laid on the sick. With friends laughing and strangers hugging all around us, our little home felt transformed into a festival dinner party, with the whole family invited and Jesus as the guest of honor.

Then I felt a grip on my shoulder. It was John. "Will you step outside with me?" he asked. I consented, and we walked through the courtyard gate and into the street. The sounds of prayer and singing hung above us, blessing the harbor breeze as it wafted by.

"I have some news for you, Priscilla." *Good news? Bad news?* I couldn't read John's face at all.

"I must go to Rome. Paul is in prison again."

"But—we still need you here! The refugee situation is getting better, but people are still starving. Jews and Gentiles are still fighting, and that's getting worse. Ours is the only house left that has both. Do you have to leave *now?*"

"No, but soon. In a few days. Your sister's son and daughter will be joining me on the journey—I must wait for them to arrive here first."

"Then—I suppose I'm going to Rome, too. Aquila is banished from the city, not me." *Long story.*

John stepped in close, and held my shoulders in his steady hands. "No, my sister. You are needed here—in this city. In this house."

We stood still for a long moment, while I stared blankly, straight ahead at his throat. He let go of my shoulders, so I grabbed his forearms and looked up into eyes. They looked even more tender than usual.

"Does Paul need you more than I do? He's been in prison lots of times. I've never been—" I gripped his arms with all my might, and tried to steady my breath.

"I know, dear Sister. This time is different. Nero is losing his mind. He's just executed his own wife, and two of his cousins. There's no telling what he'll do next. Don't hold on too tightly, Priscilla—I am called away."

"But—" I sputtered. I lost my grip on his arms, and nearly lost my grip on everything else. "You can't leave now! What about my promise?"

"Your promise?"

"My children!"

"You were promised children?"

"Yes! The Baptizer—at the Jordan. He promised me children. 'Many will call you mother' he said."

John's face relaxed knowingly. "Indeed," he replied. "Many will."

"But *when?*" I pleaded. "I'm fifty-two years old, John! I thought I was like Hannah—and the Baptizer was my Eli.[43] But it wasn't him. Then I thought Paul was my Eli, but it wasn't him. And now you—"

"Priscilla—listen." John embraced me fully, and we both fell quiet. I waited for him to speak, but he said nothing. We just stood there in the street and listened together. The sounds from the courtyard returned to my ears. Jews and Gentiles. Men and women. Grandparents and infants. Public officials and day-laborers.

---

[43] See 1 Samuel 1:2-2:21

Singing in unison.

What is man, that you are mindful of him
Or the son of man, that you care for him?
You made him a little lower than the angels!
You crowned him with glory and honor!

Warm and gentle tears flowed down my cheeks, and I stepped away to cover my face. After a moment, John leaned in and whispered, "Your children are here. They're all around you."

Suddenly I heard myself laughing. Incredulously, but freely, still wetting the front of John's tunic with my tears. *My children.* Human beings of every kind—one in the Messiah. *And behold, the woman who was barren has borne seven children.*

John released me and stepped back to look me full in the face. "Sing, barren one, who has not given birth," he quoted. "Burst into singing and shout, you who have not travailed. For more are the children of the desolate than the children of the fertile one." John put his hand on my shoulder, and kissed me on the cheek.

"Now let me go—and you'll see me return." [44] I watched him walk away, until he turned a corner and disappeared from sight. A raindrop hit my nose, and I stood there for a long moment, just to breathe. *We need the rain,* I thought. Then I returned to the courtyard, and sang with the whole of my being. One drop of rain followed another, until they added a steady percussion to our praise.

Let us fear ADONAI our God who gives the rain in its season
The autumn rain and the spring rain, and keeps the weeks appointed
for the harvest! [45]

Sow the seeds of righteousness and reap in accord with covenant love

---

[44] John is quoting Jesus (John 20:17) and the angels at his Ascension (Acts 1:11).
[45] Jeremiah 5:24

For it is time to seek ADONAI who showers righteousness on us all! [46]

Before the song was over, we were standing in a downpour—but no one moved. No one rushed for cover. Not one of us paused our singing, but lifted our voices to the skies to declare the glory of his handiwork—in Creation, in Salvation, and in us.

Omer 44 | Monday

My writing table is now back where it belongs, and that is where I spent my entire morning, and most of the afternoon. I like to start the day with my letter to Rome, then switch to translating for James and Jude when I need a change of pace. Turns out it's easier to know what other letters are trying to say, than to know what I want my own to say. But it's still challenging work. By mid-morning, Jude was finished, so I went back to my own writing.

I need to find a succinct and winning way to prove that Jesus is the one and only Messiah. *Simple right? I should have been finished by lunch time.* Here's the trick: I have to speak to so many different people at once, showing that Jesus is greater than the angels (for the Essenes), greater than Moses (for the circumsizers) and sufficient to atone for sins once and for all (for everyone).

I also need to write about sacrifice in a way that makes Jews think about the Holy of Holies, and yet connects with Gentiles who were raised with the gods and sacrifices of the Pantheon. Thankfully, every faith I know of associates blood with covenant. Every religion employs types and shadows—symbols pointing to a greater reality. Let me scribble something about that here, to get the words flowing:

> *Apart from the shedding of blood there is no forgiveness. Therefore it was necessary for the replicas of these heavenly things to be purified*

---

[46] Hosea 10:12

with these sacrifices—but the heavenly things themselves with better
sacrifices than these. For Messiah did not enter into a sanctuary made
with human hands—counterparts of the true things—but into heaven
itself, now to appear in God's presence on our behalf.

Suddenly, Demetrius popped in to pick up another batch of tents. I apologized for the shortfall, but he waved it off. "The need is less, so the supply is less. God always provides."

"Do you think God provide me some lunch now?" I quipped.

Demetrius paused and looked at my desk. "It's hard to eat with a pen in your hand," he winked on his way out the door. He knows me too well.

Omer 45 | Tuesday

It was a quiet day at home, alternating between sewing and writing. Aquila and I had just finished dinner, and sent our remaining volunteers home, when Demetrius stopped in as usual to pick up our completed tents.

"Here's eight," Aquila said, as he handed him the stack.

"Well, that's a shame," Demetrius said.

"I know. We're making fewer every day."

"That's not what I meant," Demetrius replied with a smile. "We only need seven. It's a shame I didn't tell you that before."

"Just seven?" I exclaimed. "No problem—that means we'll have one less to make tomorrow."

"Not exactly. We're done."

"Done?" Aquila and I both exclaimed.

"Yes, we have all we need. Some people are even starting to give them back. Now I have to figure out what to do with the surplus."

I don't know why we were so surprised at this news. It was going to end eventually, why not now? Demetrius embraced us both with his thanks, and promised to notify our volunteers and come back tomorrow to pick up the leftover materials. Then he walked out and left us there in the middle of our *former* tent factory. We just stood there in silence, staring at the final yellow tent on the floor between us.

"Done," I said, incredulously. "What now?"

A curious smile grew beneath Aquila's fluffy beard. "I have an idea."

Dusk was setting in as we completed our hike halfway up Mount Koressos. With a few light bags strapped to our backs, we made our way to a clearing on the northwest side of the mountain.

"Here's the spot," Aquila said, and we dropped our packs. "Tent or fire?"

He didn't even have to ask. I've always loved spreading out and arranging the tents we make, even after working on them all day. I busied myself with the stakes and ropes, while Aquila gathered kindling and chopped down a small tree nearby with his axe. As he worked, he deposited the wood into a circle of rocks.

"Have you camped here before?" I asked him.

"Who do you think put these rocks here?" he asked me with a grin. I finished the tent and placed some bedding inside. Then I wandered just past Aquila's campfire-in-progress, where I found a small granite overlook. The sun had barely kissed the horizon to my left, and the colors set the clouds aflame in the sky above and the bay below.

Ahead of me was the harbor entrance, and to my right spread the great city of Ephesus, with oil lamps beginning to flicker on in the Arcadian Way, the bathhouses, the Theatre and the Agora. Mount Pion stood tall and black above the sparkling panorama, marked only by the guardlamps on the wall which ran up one side and down the other.

"I've never been up here at night," I said.

Aquila came up gently behind me and hugged me around the waist. "Something else, isn't it?"

I could hear the fire cracking and spitting—consuming the kindling as a snack before the main course. After a long moment, we sat down together on a ledge and drank in the scene, with the city before us and the campfire behind us. I found our house and pointed it out. Then I put my head on his shoulder, and for the better part of an hour we sat still, and watched the stars come out.

"Aquila—I really need to apologize."

"No you don't."

"Yes, I do. I listened to Nicolas when he tried to make me resent you. He served me his poison and I drank it up. Maybe we don't have children because I'm barren. Or maybe I lack faith. Or maybe *you* lack faith. It's that last one—that's the one I've stuck with nine times out of ten. And lately the idea has so consumed me that—" I choked on my words, and put my hands in my face.

"I didn't bring you up here for a confession," Aquila said.

I shook my head. "There's something else I need to tell you. John shared his news with me yesterday."

"That he's going to Rome?"

"Yes, but there was more. John oversees all these miracles—like the one at the Artemision. I thought he had one for me. For us. So I begged him not to go. In my heart of hearts, I hoped that he would bring us children, even at our age."

"Because of the Baptizer's prophecy?"

"Yes. John believes it's been fulfilled. Our children are all around us, he said."

Aquila smiled thoughtfully. "But did we raise them right?"

We sat still for a long time. We watched a ship enter the harbor, and drift all the way to the wharf. Several families with small children had exited onto the pier before he spoke again.

"Some days it hurts to watch other fathers with their little ones." He took a sharp breath and tossed a small rock into the water below. "But I found myself in my work instead—visiting the sick, caring for widows and orphans. When I bring the love of Jesus to them, I truly feel whole. I wondered if you felt the same. I was hoping that you had."

"I do. I will."

"No." He put both arms around me. "Your journey has been harder for you. I've seen that every day. You carried the Baptizer's promise so buoyantly at first, but it got heavier. Thirty-five years later, you wear it like a chain around your neck. The promise has become a burden to you."

I opened my mouth to speak, but couldn't produce any words.

"Your children were all around you from the first," Aquila continued. "This was ADONAI's gift. But what you have to let go of is something I can never understand. It's yours to grieve. And it's yours to take up again. All I can do is walk beside you." He smiled sadly. "I admit I haven't always known how to be your husband. I think I am only just learning. I'm sorry for my coldness toward you—for my ignorance. You really do deserve better."

Fresh tears began to flow. I felt free—freer than I had felt in years, to think of the children I would not have as I had wished, and to weep for them. I nodded and sniffed, and my husband leaned over to kiss me on the temple. "You know, my love—you look up to all these women of the past. Heroes of the faith, you call them. And so they are. But think of it— Sarah, Rebekah, Rachel, Leah, what are they known for?"

"They're matriarchs."

"Yes, but why?" He didn't wait for me to answer this time. "They are known as the *wives* and *mothers* of patriarchs. Then there's Hannah, Ruth, Mary—all known for their faith, but more so for being the mother of Samuel, the grandmother of David, the mother of Jesus. Esther was brave, but only as an instrument of her cousin Mordecai.

"But you, my love—you have given birth to holy words, to holy communities. Not as an accessory to a father, a son, or a husband, but as yourself. Priscilla the teacher. Priscilla the missionary."

My heart swelled so intensely, I could barely stand it. "What about Deborah?" I challenged.

110

"Alright, fine. Priscilla and Deborah! Heroines of the faith in their own right." He flashed me that every-tooth smile, then got up and added a log to the flickering embers behind us. I took the opportunity to turn away from our view of the city, and warm my face by the campfire instead. Once it was roaring again, he returned and sat down behind me.

"I thought you'd never turn your back on Ephesus," he said, taking my hands from behind.

I closed my eyes and smiled, breathing in his familiar scent as it blended with the mountain air. "Just for tonight."

Omer 46 | Wednesday

Pentecost is in four days, and it's time to prepare. It hasn't been easy, since half the churches aren't talking to the other half of the churches. And some churches aren't even talking to the half they're in. *It seems I've raised an unruly bunch.* But everyone can still agree on one thing: they all want to take part in the Pentecost celebration that's held in the Agora every year.

We spent the day in the sitting room at Gaius' house: John, Aquila, Milos, Demetrius and all the leaders of the house churches. Diotrephes facilitated, while Gaius sat propped up on a couch to consult with us, in spite of his persistent fever.

The Jews sat on one side, and the Greeks on the other, with Diotrephes and Gaius (on the couch) between them on one end, and me and my party between them on the other. No one talked across the table—John appeared to be the only one that everyone could agree to speak with directly.

Judging by the house leaders' reports, this was bound to be the largest Pentecost Ephesus had ever seen, as long as equal time and equal consideration were given to each side. Today we discussed the practical issues—the space, the food and drink, the participants, the volunteers.

Tomorrow we'll talk about Scripture readings, songs, and prayers.

I'm afraid we're going to have to put a big curtain down the center. The synagogues do it for men and women, but for us it would be Jews and Greeks. Then we'd probably need more little curtains to keep the subgroups from having to look at each other. *ADONAI have mercy. The Agora is going to look like a labyrinth.*

———————————

It was mid-afternoon when Tychicus came to the door. Everyone was shocked to see him. Tychicus is half-Jewish, and a native of Ephesus, but spent most of his adult life in Rome. Sadly, we only knew him personally for a brief time. But he's widely known among the churches as a companion of Paul, and a great encourager in the Spirit of God. If Tychicus were to sit down at this table, we'd have two people everyone would agree to talk to.

We all stood up, and embraced him in turn. Then he brought news to the group: Timothy had been released from house arrest in Smyrna. We all smiled around the table, and blessed ADONAI.

"His mother is recovering from her illness," Tychicus said, "so Timothy expects to come to you soon." Then Tychicus reached into his travel bag and pulled out a little scroll with a brown seal. "I also have a letter from Paul. It's addressed to all the Believers in Ephesus. Can it be read at Pentecost on Sunday?" Diotrephes stood up and put his hand out to receive it. Tychicus stood still and looked at him, then at Gaius, who had apparently fallen asleep. After a ponderous moment he walked over to my side of the table, and handed the letter to John. Diotrephes snorted, and sat down in a huff.

John broke the seal, and unrolled it. There were several sheets bound together. Not a short message, but much shorter than Paul's letter to Rome seven years ago. The room sat speechless as John scanned one page, then the next. Aquila broke the silence. "Will you read it to the gathering on Sunday, John?" He gave Aquila a sidelong glance, then rolled up the letter and handed it to me.

"I think Priscilla should read it," John said. Aquila nodded.

I looked at each of them in turn, then reached out for the scroll and took it.

Omer 47 | Thursday

I've wanted to talk to Apollos for over a week now, but no one has seen him. Until today. Aquila had just left to visit a sick friend near the harbor when my protégé knocked on the door.

"Apollos! Where have you been? Don't you know what's been happening?"

"Yes, but I had to think. I had to get all of this straight."

"All of what straight?"

"A few weeks ago, you said something I never stopped thinking about. You said, 'I just want you to be happy.' But I'm not. I'm not happy at all. I am a teacher of the abundant life we're promised in Jesus. But my life is nowhere near abundant. Not even with four children. Not with a hundred children."

It was as plain as if the words were written on his face. "Is this about Daphne?" I asked.

Apollos had anticipated the question. "My family in Alexandria never liked her. To this day they've refused to accept her as my wife. If I went a different way, if I found someone refined, someone respectable—someone *Jewish*—they would be thrilled."

"But Apollos—your children!"

"My children need a father who speaks joy and peace into their lives. In the Agora I am a celebrated orator, but in my own home I have nothing to say. I am like a deaf mute." He rubbed his face in weariness, then took a deep breath. "Why did our Messiah die, Priscilla, if not to achieve total grace on our behalf? Why do we go on and on about sin and

113

confession and repentance when we have a Savior who atoned for it all on the Cross? His forgiveness is complete, don't you see it? The priests sprinkled the blood of bulls and goats day after day, and year after year to win a temporary reprieve for sin, but the Lamb of God has done it once and for all!"

"That's not what that means, Apollos!" He gripped my shoulders and steered me to the couch, where we both sat down.

"It's what *you* taught me. If I—if I can't do this anymore, God will understand my weakness. I will be forgiven. No, I am forgiven in advance! Look, Priscilla—I arrived in Corinth preaching the baptism of John—sin and repent, sin and repent, sin and repent. But you showed me a higher truth. It just took me till now to understand it fully. I was mired in the economy of sin, like a pitiful debtor working off his bills in prison with no hope of release. But you broke in and showed me what it means to have *total freedom* in Jesus. The debt is canceled, the prisoner is released!"

My head was swimming, my heart pounding. How could I speak to this? Technically, he hadn't said a single thing wrong. Then the words of Gaius returned to my ears: *Look at the fruit. Look at the fruit.*

Apollos continued. "My parents were never proud of me. My family ignored me. My religion and now my marriage are drowning me in ritual obligation. The only light in all that darkness—has been you." I felt like I was watching the grandest cedar in Lebanon being chopped down before my eyes. Suddenly my spirit awoke.

"Nicolas!" I hissed.

"I'm not Nicolas!"

"I know your name, Apollos. Come with me!" I jumped up and grabbed his arm, yanking him out the door like an impertinent child. I hustled him down the Curetes and past the Agora. What a sight we must have been—a well-built man being marched through the streets of Ephesus by a little woman with fire in her eyes.

"Religion and marriage. Religion and marriage. Nicolas, you filthy serpent!" I shouted to the air. "You slither up behind us with a forked tongue between your teeth. You whisper sweet and aromatic words in our ears, but the fruit is poison! You taunt us with total grace and total freedom but you have no interest in grace—no interest in anyone's freedom but your own!"

My rant continued as we passed the Theatre. Patrons nearby stopped to watch, as if we were actors engaged in a pre-show performance. "You pay homage to Messiah but undermine his words!" I shouted. "You call yourself a simple rope dealer, I'll tell you what you are. You're an antichrist! On a mission from hell to divide and conquer the children of God. And by the ropes you use to bind the Spirit, you yourself will hang!" A few of the Theatre patrons smiled and clapped.

We turned to climb the hill beside the Theatre, flying up the steps without losing a fraction of our pace. When we arrived at the fancy wooden gates I nearly knocked poor Constantine to the ground. I was ready to tear the heretic apart.

"Where's Nicolas?" I demanded, as I stood heaving in the middle of his sitting room, with Apollos' arm still trapped in my white-knuckled grip. Zoe stepped out bravely from behind a giant urn to answer my question.

"He is traveling, madam."

"Traveling?" I asked, my chest still heaving. "Where?"

"He didn't say, madam. He left this morning."

"How far? When will he be back?"

Zoe just stared at the floor and shook her head. We marched back out, across the courtyard and through the still-open wooden gate. Once in the street again, I turned and put a finger in Apollos' face. "If you see him, don't talk. Don't listen. Come straight to me." Apollos nodded nervously.

With that I stormed off, abandoning my bewildered friend in front of the house of Nicolas, "Deacon of Jerusalem."

But this is the covenant I will make with the house of Israel after those days. I will put my Torah within them. Yes, I will write it on their heart. I will be their God and they will be my people. No longer will each teach his neighbor or each his brother, saying: "Know ADONAI," for they will all know me, from the least of them to the greatest. For I will forgive their iniquity, their sin I will remember no more.[47]

The more I prayed about it, the more convicted I became that Nicolas' argument about sacrifice is incomplete. That's why it didn't strike me as abjectly false. It's based in truth, but it omits the most important testimony: that sin is still sin. It's not *annulled* at the Cross, it's *forgiven*.

It was time to address that exact point in my letter to the Hebrews in Rome. So I picked up my reed, dipped it in ink, and prayed: *Blessed are you, ADONAI our God, King of the Universe. Behold, I come to do your will.*

By God's will we have been made holy through the offering of the body of Messiah Jesus once for all. Indeed, every priest stands day by day serving and offering the same sacrifices again and again, which can never take away sins.

But on the other hand, when this One offered for all time a single sacrifice for sins, he sat down at the right hand of God—waiting from then on, until his enemies are made a footstool for his feet. For by one offering he has perfected forever those being made holy. The Holy Spirit also testifies to us—for after saying,

"This is the covenant that I will cut with them: 'After those days,' says ADONAI, 'I will put my Torah upon their hearts, and upon their minds I will write it,'" then He says, "I will remember their sins and their lawless deeds no more."

There's the forgiveness. Now, what does it mean to have the Law written on our hearts? Does it mean we are each a law unto ourselves?

---

[47] Jeremiah 31:32ff

ADONAI forbid! Rather, we are transformed as one body to reflect the law of Jesus in the New Covenant. Jesus—the living Torah, and the green tree. So consider the fruit of that tree: [48] not chaos and division, but love and good deeds. *Write that, Priscilla.*

> *Now where there is removal of these, there is no longer an offering for sin. Therefore, brothers and sisters, we have boldness to enter into the Holy of Holies by the blood of Jesus. He inaugurated a new and living way for us through the curtain—that is, his flesh. We also have a High Priest over God's household.*

> *So let us draw near with a true heart in full assurance of faith, with hearts sprinkled clean from an evil conscience and body washed with pure water. Let us hold fast the unwavering confession of hope, for he who promised is faithful. And let us consider how to stir up one another to love and good deeds.*

Pentecost is almost here—and this is the calm before the storm. Aquila and I made certain to take a good Sabbath this evening, and clear our day tomorrow. It's not easy, but we've been trying to *create rest,* as Apollos would say. We'll need all the rest we can get before that day arrives. I have a feeling our love in Ephesus will be tested, for better or for worse.

Omer 49 | Saturday

> *I am ADONAI your God, who brought you forth out of the land of Egypt, so that you would not be their slaves, and I have broken the bars of your yoke and made you walk upright.* [49]

Today is the seventh Sabbath. The final day before Pentecost. And I almost made it till sundown before picking my reed up again to finish my letter. The task seems so daunting sometimes, it's easy to put it off. But

---

[48] See Luke 23:31 and Ezekiel 20:47
[49] Leviticus 26:13 (from the Torah portion for the week)

then I remember that the task is not my own, it belongs to God. *If the Spirit speaks through me, then I am only a scribe. His yoke is easy, and his burden is light.*

As I write, it's time for bed, and my letter is nearly finished. I followed up *love and good deeds* with a sermon on Faith. Yes, Jesus established a New Covenant, but we cannot understand the new until we comprehend the old. Contrary to the teachings of some, Salvation was *never* achieved by the Law—even under Moses—but only by Faith. The great heroes of Scripture were not saved by their good deeds, but by believing in the promise of ADONAI for the One who was yet to come. And when he came, he didn't enter the Holy Place by the power of the Law—the blood of goats and calves, but by his own blood. The Law established a Covenant, making forgiveness possible. But the Messiah, by his perfect obedience, made forgiveness an eternal reality.

Let both sides take note! You, who are disciples of the Law, and you who preach Total Grace, witness the giving of the Torah at Mount Sinai and the baptism of the Holy Spirit, coming together on the Day of Pentecost:

> *For you have not come to a mountain that can be touched, and to a blazing fire, and to darkness and gloom and storm, and to the blast of a shofar and a voice whose words made those who heard it beg that not another word be spoken to them...*

then reminded them that we now stand on the other side:

> *...but we are receiving a kingdom that cannot be shaken. So let us show thanks—through this we may offer worship in a manner pleasing to God, with reverence and awe. For our God is a consuming fire.*

Now, what does it look like when the Torah comes to be written on our hearts? What is the fruit of this covenant faith?

> *Let brotherly love continue. Do not neglect to show hospitality to strangers—for in doing so, some have entertained angels without knowing it. Remember the prisoners as if you were fellow prisoners, and*

those who are mistreated as if you also were suffering bodily. Let marriage be held in honor among all and the marriage bed kept undefiled. Keep your lifestyle free from the love of money, and be content with what you have.

But if righteousness is a gift, that still doesn't make it easy. I doubt anyone knows this better than I do. So how can I encourage my children in their struggles?

Now all discipline seems painful at the moment—not joyful. But later it yields the peaceful fruit of righteousness to those who have been trained by it.

I cautioned them to be on the lookout for Nicolases in their midst:

Also see to it that there is no immoral or godless person—like Esau, who sold his birthright for one meal.

Finally, I urged them to recommit to their leaders, because they have served faithfully. All that remained was to write my greetings at the beginning and the end, but my hand was aching. I got up from the table and laid down on the couch.

That's when Aquila walked into the room. "Did you read Paul's letter to the Ephesians yet?"

I sat up again. "No—I can't believe I forgot!"

"Well, I just finished it."

"What did he want to talk to us about?"

"Religion and marriage," Aquila smirked.

"Really?"

"And unity among Believers. Here, listen." He sat down and cleared his throat. "'This mystery is that the Gentiles are joint heirs and fellow members of the same body and co-sharers of the promise in Messiah Jesus through the Good News.'"

"Now there's a timely message."

"There's more in here about unity—for us," Aquila added. 'Husbands, love your wives just as Messiah also loved his church and gave himself up for her to make her holy, having cleansed her by immersion in the Word.' He goes on about this, and ends with 'This mystery is great—but I am talking about Messiah and the Church. In any case, let each of you love his own wife as himself...'" he trailed off.

"And?"

"Yes, there are some instructions to wives, too. But that's not really for me to read."

I took the scroll out of his hand, to pick up where he left off.

"...and let the wife respect her husband," I read aloud. Aquila blushed, and I laughed at him.

"You don't have to say it," he told me bashfully.

"I want to say it." I made him look at me. "I respect you, Aquila."

"And I love you, Priscilla." We laughed at ourselves at first, but then he put his hand on my face. His eyes were deep and warm, just like his voice. "My beautiful Priscilla. I love you as myself."

It was time to turn in, so I stepped outside to extinguish the lamp. But when I opened the door, I almost tripped over a sullen figure, waiting by the door, his head buried between his knees. He turned his face and glanced up at me with red, puffy eyes.

"Apollos!" I cried. "What's happened?"

Aquila rushed to his side, then gently helped him to his feet. Apollos embraced Aquila like a drowning man, sobbing violently into his shoulder. After regaining his breath he repeated the words "I'm sorry," again and again and again.

Aquila led our friend inside, then over to the couch to lay him down. He put a pillow under his head, took off his sandals, and put his feet up. I found a towel for a handkerchief and handed it to him. In due time, my husband took a seat next to me, across from the couch, and spoke.

"Can you talk about it?"

Apollos wiped his face. "It's my parents," he muttered. "They've been killed. At sea." He hid his face in the towel.

"Oh, Apollos. Oh, Apollos." Aquila closed his eyes and began praying softly in the Spirit. Apollos removed the cloth from his face again, and folded it carefully. Then he sat up with his elbows on his knees.

"We were never close. I think you know that."

"It's hard to lose your parents, Apollos. I'm sure you loved them."

"Maybe, but it's not even about that. I just—" He tried to take another deep breath, but it caught halfway. "I always thought I would have another chance. Another opportunity to make them proud of me. But now I never will. That hope is sunk forever—resting with them at the bottom of the sea."

Aquila prayed a bit more, and spoke again. "We—Priscilla and I—we are *so* proud of you. There is no greater blessing than to—"

"You're too kind."

"I assure you it's sincere."

"No!" Apollos stood up and started pacing the room. "You've been the father that my father never was, and this community is the family that my family never was. But I've betrayed you all. Call me Judas!"

"Apollos. You are already forgiven. You could never do anything to make us hate you."

"You don't even know what I've done!"

"Did you—" I interjected. Apollos couldn't even look at me. "Is Daphne—" my question failed, but it didn't matter. Apollos hung his head, then shook it slowly. *He didn't go through with it.* A rush of bitter relief flowed through my veins. *Don't show it, Priscilla. Stay in the moment.* Aquila saw me struggling, and bailed me out.

"You are no Judas, my brother." Aquila sat down next to him. "You have been ill-used. You were ill-used as a child, and you've been ill-used these past few weeks. By Nicolas."

That name. It changes the air in a room whenever it's uttered. Aquila continued. "I can only speak this way because I've had no encounter with him. If I had—ADONAI only knows. But greater is the One *who is in you,*

121

Apollos."

Aquila continued speaking, but Apollos' words continued to echo in my head, drowning him out: *You've been the father that my father never was.* Which begs the question—have I been the mother? After all, I taught him. I guided him. I loved him unconditionally. I even fed him. And then he grew up.

I was a mother. I had a son.

I never knew.

PENTECOST

Omer 50: Pentecost Sunday

And when the day of Pentecost was fully come, they were all with one accord in one place. [50]

Well, they put up a curtain after all, splitting the Agora right down the middle, and I could barely hold my tongue I was so furious. *So much for being "with one accord."* At least nobody demanded smaller curtains to subdivide the Jews and the Greeks amongst themselves. One curtain was already too many.

Aquila and I arrived at dawn, and watched the others come streaming in. Worship was set to begin at the third hour, but by the second hour we were already enjoying the company of Demetrius and Thea, Tychicus, Xanthe, Spiros, and Basil. Tassos and Lyra (the clothing merchants) joined us by accident, forgetting that the Agora was closed today. But they stayed anyway.

One surprising arrival was Tertius, who served as Paul's scribe for the letter to the Romans, [51] and was just recently made Bishop of Iconium. He also served with me in the Seventy, all those years ago. I embraced him enthusiastically, and Aquia greeted him with a snide remark. "Where's your litter?" he winked. "I didn't think bishops were allowed to do their own walking." Tertius blushed and smiled. He knows that Aquila doesn't tease anyone unless he's proud of them.

Next I saw Marcus himself, arriving with a small entourage. I almost wanted to laugh, because they were trying to look dignified, but obviously they had no idea what they'd gotten themselves into. Shortly after that, Diotrephes and a number of house church leaders arrived. Apollos, John and Milos were noticeably absent. Nicolas, I assumed, was still traveling. In his stead I saw his house-servants, Zoe and Constantine—probably

---

[50] Acts 2:1 (Although the book of Acts had not been written yet, snippets like this would surely have been in circulation by this time, through oral tradition.)
[51] Romans 16:22

freed up by his absence.

With still more than a half-hour to go, the Agora was filling up rapidly. Large numbers of refugees were piling in, no doubt attracted to the mountains of donated food and clothing left over from the Artemision ten days ago. And some of it was fresh—a seemingly inexhaustible abundance that no one could quite explain. The ever-growing crowd of newcomers brought an unforeseen side-effect. The more they showed up, the more we had to shorten the curtain at the opposite end from the platform, thus creating a larger and larger "undivided" area at the back.

"It's the third hour—time to start." Diotrephes commanded. "Where's the Elder?" John had been slated to moderate the gathering, but nobody knew where he was. Without him, the fragile social balance we'd achieved would be in jeopardy.

I stepped up onto the edge of the platform, and looked out into the marketplace. People were still streaming in from every corner. If this continued, there would be no place left to stand. The crowd's expectant chatter alone was almost deafening. They kept pressing and jostling the curtain to make way. *Why doesn't someone just tear it down?* I fumed inwardly. But now it seemed the curtain was the least of our worries.

"We have a different problem," I said to Aquila. He nodded with pursed lips, gazing into the growing throng. Then I saw Marcus walk up to speak to Diotrephes, who subsequently turned to hush the crowd.

"I've been informed that this gathering is too large for the Agora; we are being relocated to the Amphitheatre. Please follow the guards' instructions, in an orderly fashion, and we will begin as soon as everyone is settled in our new location."

The city guards took twenty to thirty people at a time, from front to back with no concern for which side of the curtain they were standing on, and marched us down the Curetes Way, around the base of Mount Pion and through the Theatre gates. Many had already begun a song of praise, and for an hour or so the party became a parade, complete with singing, dancing and shouting in every known language.

The guards took upon themselves the role of usher at the Theatre, seating everyone in the order they arrived, The mood was dampened considerably as every row and every section contained a tense mix of irritable sectarians, filtered into a sizeable cohort of the blissfully ignorant. Naturally, some hardliners still managed to find their way to the far left of the great bowl, and some to the far right. But the rest were jumbled up like storm-tossed shells on a beach.

I started looking for John again. It was already the fourth hour. *Does he do this on purpose?* Just then I noticed Milos, jogging through the northern Theatre gate and heading straight for Aquila and me. "John is—" he put his hands on his knees, bent over and held up a finger. After catching his breath, he straightened up and delivered the news. "John has departed."

"Departed? What do you mean?" Aquila asked. The leaders had spotted Milos by now, and were gathering around.

"He's boarding a ship for Rome. Priscilla—your niece and nephew came to his house at the second hour this morning. They arrived on a ship from Tyre to Rome, with only a cargo stop in Ephesus."

"Hadassah's children? They were here?" I exclaimed.

"The captain granted them just two hours to collect John and bring him back, before he pushed off again. They send their fondest greetings, Priscilla. And their regrets."

"John isn't coming at all?" Demetrius stated the obvious. Milos shook his head, still huffing.

Demetrius and Aquila stepped aside to discuss what they should do. Milos' glanced at me, leaned forward, and put a tiny scroll in my hand.

"Here, John left a letter behind for you personally."

I ran my finger across the red wax seal that bore the monogram of

John, son of Zebedee. Then I looked back at Milos. "Why didn't you go with him?"

"He said it was my choice."

I smirked at him. "That's what he always says."

"I know. But if I'm going to travel, I thought I might go back and visit Capernaum instead." He winked at me, and I laughed. *Ana.*

Diotrephes cut in. "Do not worry, my brothers and sisters," he said with a subtle grin. "John will be missed, but we all know what to do. Come—let's begin."

Diotrephes strode out to the center of the circular stage, with some twenty-thousand souls teetering over him, expecting something, but not knowing what. He signaled to three men on his left, in full Jewish regalia, and they lifted long shofars to their lips. With a triumphant blast, the crowd quieted. Pentecost had begun.

"Welcome to Pentecost—Shavu'ot—in the Great Theatre of the great city of Ephesus!" Cheers and applause erupted from the audience. Praises arose in Greek, Hebrew, Aramaic and dozens of other tongues. "My name is Diotrephes."

"Diotrephes the Greek!" three voices shouted in unison, from the far right side of the Theatre. Diotrephes sputtered.

"I assure you, my brothers and sisters, that I am the one properly appointed to—"

"We were promised equal time!" more voices demanded. "Aquila should lead!" another said. *Is this who we are? Who we've become? A cracked assemblage of makeshift components, all vying for dominance? An open forum for every ambitious narcissist to shout his demands into the void?* I looked at Aquila, sitting next to me with his head in his hands. Trying to be invisible. Meanwhile, more voices bickered back and forth.

"Gaius is ill, so Diotrephes is our leader!"

"No! We want Aquila!"

"Diotrephes!"

"Aquila!"

My head was swooning with bad memories of the Riot at the Artemision. Except this time, it would be entirely perpetrated by Believers. The Ephesian church would never, ever hear the end of it.

That was the moment Nicolas appeared. Nobody saw him come in, but there he was—standing center-stage with one arm around Diotrephes, and the other arm held up to calm the crowd.

"It's Nicolas of Pergamum. Let him speak!" one group shouted.

"Pay your respect to the Deacon of Jerusalem!" the opposing group responded. Everyone seemed to think he was on their side.

"Thank you, my brothers and sisters. My name is Nicolas. Before I speak, please let me say that Diotrephes was simply carrying out his duty. And I believe he has done so quite admirably in Gaius' absence, has he not?" A tepid applause followed, then Nicolas politely gestured to Diotrephes to step away, and give him some space.

"Secondly!" he smiled broadly to the crowd. "I must say that, not only is this the largest Pentecost celebration Ephesus has ever seen, I believe it to be the largest gathering of Believers ever to occur outside Jerusalem! Surely that deserves a moment of recognition, Yes?"

A cheer went up, as thousands and thousands of participants applauded for themselves. Then a chant arose, "Great is the Church of the Ephesians! Great is the Church of the Ephesians!" The chant continued for several moments. Then Nicolas motioned for silence again.

"This is a very special moment for us. Let me begin by—"

"Why are *you* here?" an especially vocal member from the front of the audience demanded. "You don't belong to Ephesus. Where is The Elder?" He turned to face the assembly and demanded. "We want The Elder! We want The Elder!"

"John has departed!" Nicolas shot back, before collecting himself.

128

"John has left us, for Rome. He will not be returning. I have come to shepherd you in his stead. Now! Before you object—allow me to bear witness to something truly troubling in this church. This may be the largest assembly of Believers the city has ever seen. But it's also the most sharply divided. Tell me—would Jesus have tolerated that curtain in the Agora?" Murmurs arose and heads shook mournfully. Nicolas shot a glance at me, and my cheeks burned.

"Even here, mixed together in the Great Theatre, we do not have unity. This is not what Jesus came to do. This is not what Jesus died to achieve!" The crowd was silent. I was fidgeting. *Wherever he's taking this, it can't be good. Somebody should stop him.*

"Remember the ascension of Jesus! Before he departed, he sent us forth to Jerusalem, Judea, Samaria and the ends of the earth. Then he left us behind to be his people, his own body on the earth. But that was only the beginning! He has something much greater than mortal humanity in store for us. After all, did Jesus not say, "You are all *gods?*"[52]

"Some of you say there was one Messiah, and others say there shall be a second, but I give you a new word—a word that breaks the chains of this deathly religion that restrains and divides you.

"The new word is this: There is not one Messiah, nor are there two. There are many Messiahs. Thousands. Millions! How can this be, you ask? Because the arch-prophet Jesus came from heaven, not to save us, but to empower every one of us to *save ourselves.* This is God's abundant life, and nothing else. My brothers and sisters—we will be whole again when we declare this truth: We are all Messiahs!"

There it is, finally, in black and white. Blasphemy.

I watched in horror as the Theatre exploded with joy. Worshippers jumped up and down, thrust their hands in the air and cheered at the

---

[52] This is a genuine quote of Jesus (John 10:33), who is, in turn, quoting Psalm 82:6. But Nicolas is using this statement to put himself and his hearers on equal footing with Jesus. Jesus, however, is pointing out an inconsistency between the Pharisees' beliefs and their objections to his own claim to be the Son of God.

news that every standard had been abolished.

But then another voice pierced the chaos. "Antichrist!" The charge emerged from somewhere within the crowd. It must have been shouted in unison by a hundred people.

"Antichrist!" it came again. A single voice, but an exceptionally loud one. I strained to see where it was coming from. Then I noticed a small group entering through the gate at the far corner of the stage, and at the center of that group—was Gaius! He leaned heavily on Isadora, but marched steadfastly toward Nicolas, his arm and finger outstretched. The crowd was stunned to silence.

"Woe to the one who denies that Jesus is the Messiah—the Christ—the only begotten Son of God! This one is the antichrist!"

"Gaius—" Nicolas stammered. "It's wonderful to see you feeling—"

"Silence, you viper!" He now stood at the edge of the stage, in full view of the gathering. When the fever left Gaius' head, the fire must have gone straight to his bones. "Every word you speak brings another soul down with you!"

"Long live Gaius!" a smattering of voices shouted from the crowd.

Gaius ignored them. "We know your deeds, Nicolas. We know the spells you put on Diotrephes, and others," he said. I breathed again. Diotrephes held his place in the center of the stage mopping his forehead. Next to him was Nicolas, his lips thinning and his eyes narrowing.

Gaius continued to gather strength, and stepped away from Isadora. He took a few more steps under his own power and gestured toward the crowd. "These people have toiled in patient endurance to serve thousands upon thousands of perishing souls, but you! No, you do not lift a finger, and what is more, you divide them up until they can accomplish nothing as a body—starved of the very Spirit that gives them life and breath."

His evil will be exposed before the assembly.

Nicolas bent his lips into a smile. "Please brother Gaius, I am certain that—"

"I said do not speak! Only listen. Your total freedom and total grace are nothing more than a noose around the people's neck. And who is holding the other end of that rope? You call yourself an apostle, but I have declared what you truly are. You are an antichrist!" Nicolas—perhaps for the first time in his life—was speechless. He held still and received the onslaught, with his mouth open, like the rest of us.

Then came the distant sound of boots marching. Quietly at first, then louder. A buzz of anxiety and fear began to spread, as a century of Roman soldiers stomped through the northern gate—armed and clad to quell an uprising.

The soldiers filed percussively onto the stage, then stomped to attention. A centurion on horseback trotted from behind, around the phalanx and into the center where Nicolas and Diotrephes stood, now visibly shaking. Gaius leaned again on Isadora.

"Who is responsible for this assembly?" the centurion barked in their direction. Nicolas and Diotrephes pointed in unison to Gaius. Three officers dragged him into the center.

"We have been watching you!" the centurion declared. "And listening to the sounds of rebellion from this Theatre. By order of the Roman consul—" the officer paused ominously, and glanced at a shadowy figure to his right, mounted on a pale horse in full regalia. His face was concealed by a wide-brimmed hat, so that only his snowy beard was visible. The man nodded slowly, so the centurion resumed his edict. "—I hereby disperse this assembly! You have till the count of fifty. All who remain will be apprehended!"

The captain to his left took a deep breath and bellowed his count for all to hear. *"One! Two! Three!"*

"This is no rebellion!" Gaius insisted. "It is no riot! We have dismissed the agitator, and wish to remain and worship!"

"Silence!" The centurion commanded. "Not another peep from you." I looked over at Nicolas, who was smirking now.

131

The captain continued his count, trying desperately to make every number heard. *"Four! Five! Six!"*

"If I could only have a word—" Gaius begged, but the centurion was serious. He nodded to a soldier who unsheathed a club. I watched him cock it above his head, ready to smash Gaius' knees to pieces.

I lunged toward him in a panic, but Aquila reached out and gripped me tightly in his arms. "No, my love!"

The captain counted on. *"Seven! Eight! Nine!"* But before the officer could swing his club, his wrist was crushed in the grip of a massive hand from behind him. He screamed in agony as the club hit the ground. When I looked again, I saw that the hand belonged to a herculean sailor with a broken jaw. *Poseidon!*

In a heartbeat the soldiers marched into action to issue a counterattack. But before they could engage the assailant, dozens of shipmates rushed in to surround Poseidon, with Captain Briarus himself standing resolutely at his side.

"Ten! Eleven! Twelve!" Three officers took advantage of the diversion, to drag Gaius out from under the melee and hustle him toward the southern gate. *"Thirteen! Fourteen! Fifteen!"*

Poseidon stood head and shoulders above the entire scene. It occurred to me in a flash that Poseidon and every one of his mates from Cyprus were probably homeless now. And yet, here they were, helping *us*. Poseidon turned to face the stands and thundered, "Men of Ephesus! *Noble* men and women of Ephesus!" He glanced at me, and every nerve in my body shimmered with pride. Then he resumed his battle cry. "Will you let thugs of Rome steal your captain away?"

"Sixteen! Seventeen! Eighteen!" Scores of Greek worshippers began to filter down from the stands in response to Poseidon's call. They promptly linked arms to block the southern gate in front of the soldiers. "If you take Gaius, you must take us." The soldiers did a quick about-face and made for the northern gate, where hundreds of Jewish Believers were already standing with arms folded across their chests.

"Nineteen! Twenty! Twenty-one!"

"This is intolerable!" the centurion shrieked into the crowd, with spittle forming in one corner of his lips. "Every one of you who defies this company stands in defiance of Caesar himself! There will be no mercy, mark my words!"

A breeze began to blow in from the harbor, which quickly grew in strength. In no time it had whipped up into a gale force wind, forcing the crowd into their seats, and the soldiers onto their knees. Shields were turned to the west to block the assault. Tall waves could be seen in the water, crested with foam and lashing out at the hapless boats docked at the wharf.

Then, nothing. In an instant the wind was gone. In the silence, one worshipper in the center of the Theatre could be heard like a pealing bell, praying aloud in the Spirit. Then those around him, and then those around them. Within moments a heavenly chorus of praying voices had filled the bowl to the brim, echoing back and forth in angelic polyphony. The pitch rose, then rose again, until a single voice pierced through in Latin, in a most unexpected way.

"Luciana, daughter of Tacitus!"

The beleaguered centurion cocked his head. "Who said that?"

"Twenty-two! Twenty-three! Twenty-four! Twenty-five!" Even the counting captain paused for a curious moment, to see who might answer the challenge.

"Luciana, daughter of Tacitus!" the voice insisted.

"Whoever speaks the name Luciana, come and face me!" he ordered. A moment later, a woman in the crowd left her party behind and descended the steps to stand calmly in front of the centurion. It was Zoe.

The captain resumed his task. *"Twenty-six! Twenty-seven! Twenty-eight!"*

"You! What do you know about Luciana?"

"Only that she loved you." Zoe smiled.

"Twenty-nine!"

Next I heard the voice of Constantine, this time in Iberian:
"Esmeralda of Cordoba!"

"*Thirty!*"

Then an unknown voice, in Aramaic: "Martelle of Antioch!"

"*Thirty-one!*"

And another, in Greek: "Eudora, daughter of Euripides!"

"*Thirty-two! Thirty-three! Thirty-four!*"

A sword clattered noisily on the stone, as the chorus of prayers continued in the background. "That's my mother," said one voice from among the formation. Then two, then four. Dozens of names came pouring out of the crowd, and more and more infantrymen dropped their shoulders, their shields and their weapons. Some headed straight for the exit. Some collapsed to the ground and wept. But the captain remained to continue his count.

"*Thirty-five! Thirty-six! Thirty-seven! Thirty-eight!*"

The centurion shook his fist and dismounted his horse. "What devilry is this?" he demanded. He paced back and forth like a caged lion, until he stood face-to-face with Gaius, now freed from his bonds.

"*Thirty-nine! Forty! Forty-one! Forty-two!*"

Gaius put his hand on the centurion's iron shoulder plate. "As I said before, this is no rebellion, and no riot. This is Pentecost. Shavu'ot. An appointed time for Jews—and now for all Believers in the Messiah of Israel—to welcome the Spirit of the One True God into our midst."

"*Forty-three! Forty-four! Forty-five!*"

The centurion lowered his face to meet that of Gaius, and whispered. "How do you know our mothers' names?"

"*Forty-six!*"

"We don't. The Spirit of God has shown us."

"*Forty-seven!*"

"But why?"

"*Forty-eight!*"

"That we were not shown."

134

"Forty-nine!" the captain insisted.

"Will you please *shut up?"* the centurion turned and barked. He glared at the captain while gesturing at the crowd. "Not one soul has dispersed! We can't arrest them all, can we Rufus?" The captain widened his eyes, and held his peace.

The centurion removed his helmet and took a step closer to Gaius, gazing at him with eyes like glass. "No one has uttered my mother's name since I was a boy. She was killed by my grandfather, whose name you apparently also know. It was a matter of family honor, he told us."

"What is *your* name?" John asked tenderly.

"I am Tacitus Nestorius."

"You are a courageous man, Nestorius. In your training you are hardened like steel against the fear of any foe. But there is one fear you have not mastered. You are afraid of your own heart."

Aquila picked up my bag, took out the letter from Paul and handed it to me. "Read it now," he said. Gaius had taken Nestorius aside to speak privately, and the prayers of the congregation were growing quiet. I breathed a prayer of courage, and stepped out to center stage. All the soldiers were gone. I opened the scroll, cleared my throat, and looked up at the throng towering over me.

"I am Priscilla!" I declared. "Here in my hand—"

"Mother Priscilla!" someone shouted. I tried not to let anything distract me.

"I stand before you today to read—"

"Mother Priscilla! Speak to your children!" Not from one voice, but many. I cleared my throat a second time. "I have here a letter from our brother, the Apostle Paul, who is in chains in Rome: 'Paul, an apostle of Messiah Jesus by God's will, to the Believers in Ephesus—those trusting in Messiah Jesus: grace and *shalom* to you, from God our Father and our Lord Jesus the Messiah!'"

And together, as one, we listened. Everyone knew Paul. To receive a letter from him, just for us, was a signature honor. The letter itself was a masterpiece. And it addressed so many of the issues we were battling. He wrote to us of the great supremacy of Jesus: "God placed all things under Messiah's feet and appointed him as head over all things for his community."

And the centrality of faith: "For by grace you have been saved through faith. And this is not from yourselves—it is the gift of God. It is not based on deeds, so that no one may boast."

And the unity of Jew and Gentile: "For Jesus is our *shalom*, the One who made the two into one and broke down the middle wall of separation—for through him we both have access to the Father by the same Spirit." I was so thankful to have that blasted curtain behind us.

And then a message that hit me right between my eyes. "Be angry, but do not sin. Do not let the sun go down on your anger." I thought about Nicolas. "Get rid of all bitterness and rage and anger and quarreling and slander, along with all malice. Instead, be kind to one another, compassionate, forgiving each other just as God in Messiah also forgave you."

When the letter was done, I handed it back to Aquila. I breathed deeply and looked at the expectant faces in the crowd. Then I looked at Gaius, who smiled with his eyes and bowed his head ever so slightly toward me. *Now for the sermon.* Twenty-five thousand people were at full attention to hear this diminutive woman's interpretation of a letter from a spiritual giant.

"We must walk in love, not fear! Not fear of heresy or heretics, of accusers or accusations." I saw quiet heads bobbing up and down all across the Theatre. "Let us move forward in faith—a true faith that has paved our way to salvation from the days of Abel[53] onward. Let us go forward as one body, in the freedom to do right! Let us be imitators of

---

[53] Hebrews 11:4

God in the Messiah. Let us go from this place, and—as the Apostles say—walk in love."

"My children! Let these words not return empty. Gaius spoke passionately in the Spirit to Nicolas; he also spoke accurately. But now—and I believe I speak for Gaius, as well as all leaders of this church—I must say something different. Nicolas, we forgive you." A ripple of gasps, praises and curses filtered through the crowd. "Make no mistake! Your platform here is gone forever, and your falsehoods bear consequences of their own. But we do not hold it against you.

I listened as my words of forgiveness were slowly met with amens and cheers of encouragement. A final charge was needed. A clarion call. So I lifted my arms to heaven and shouted with all my strength, "Wake up, O sleeper!" The crowd applauded and cried and sang their praises as I finished the benediction. "Wake up, O sleeper! Rise from the dead, and Jesus our Messiah will shine on you all!"

Pentecost Monday [54]

I shall restore to you the years that the locust has eaten
You will surely eat and be satisfied
and praise the name of ADONAI your God.
So it will be afterward, I will pour out my Spirit on all flesh
your sons and daughters will prophesy
your old men will dream dreams
your young men will see visions
Also on the male and the female servants
will I pour out my Spirit in those days.
I will show wonders in the heavens and on the earth—

---

[54] Pentecost Monday, also known as "Whit Monday" or "Holy Spirit Monday" is recognized primarily in the Anglican, Eastern Orthodox and Roman Catholic Traditions. In the latter, it is observed as the Memorial of the Blessed Virgin Mary, Mother of the Church.

blood, fire and pillars of smoke.
Then all who call on the name of ADONAI will be saved.[55]

I'm afraid it was almost lunch time today when we finally stood to our feet and put on our clothes. The events of yesterday began in the morning, but they did not end until very late. An account of all that transpired might fill a book on its own. Another time.

Once my eyes were clear, I sat back down at my writing table to finish my work. The letters of James and Jude were now fully translated into Greek. I called for Aquila to asked him to copy them for me while I completed my letter to the Hebrews in Rome. All that remained were the opening and closing greetings. As I've said before, all my letters in the past have been to my own relatives, or to individual brothers and sisters in the church. I've never written anything like this before, so I decided to borrow Paul's method of greeting an audience, and adapt it for myself.

I got out a fresh page, and started at the top:

Priscilla, a servant of Messiah Jesus, called to be a teacher and set apart for the good news of ADONAI, which he announced beforehand through his prophets in the Scriptures. Concerning his Son, who is greater than Moses, greater than angels and sits at the right hand of the Father—the seed of David and high priest forever in the order of Melchizedek. To Junia and the Hebrews in Rome, loved by God, called to be disciples: grace to you and shalom from God our Father and Jesus the Messiah!

I wrote the last word with a flourish, and set the page aside. "Too much?" I asked Aquila, who had arrived to look over my shoulder.

"Just right."

For the record, I don't think Nicolas is a devil—though he was certainly influenced by one. By John and Gaius' definition, he is an antichrist, which is a highly influential, but badly deluded human being—

---

[55] Excerpts from Joel chapter 2

created in the image of ADONAI, and redeemed (if he would accept it) by the blood of the Lamb. But once a man like this has tasted the heavenly gift of enlightenment, become a partaker of the Holy Spirit and the powers of the world to come, then fallen away? I doubt he will ever humble himself enough to repent.[56] But thankfully, that's not up to me.

Although Nicolas is not a demon, he does have a way of appearing and disappearing that no one quite understands. By the time I got back to my seat to express my forgiveness to Nicolas personally, he was long gone. No one saw him leave, and no one saw him the rest of the day or night. My premonition is that he'll avoid Ephesus for a long time. However, that doesn't mean his devoted followers—who are being called Nicolaitans—will make themselves quite so scarce. I have a feeling we'll continue to find them haunting the bathhouses of the city, if any of us cares to look.

Now for the closing greeting. After looking back over my letter to Rome, I estimate 5,000 words, which is well under the 7,000 that were in Paul's. I figured I should point this out at the end—except without the arithmetic. Or the comparison to Paul.

I urge you, brothers and sisters, listen patiently to this word of exhortation, for in fact I have written to you in few words.

It could have been longer. So much longer.

When my brothers and sisters from Italy learned that I was working on a letter to Rome, they insisted that I share their greetings. I wrote them all down on little slips of paper, which I finally got out to look through. I counted thirty-nine, which was too many to mention individually, so I had to generalize.

Lastly, they'll want to hear the good news about Timothy. If he's able

---

[56] See Hebrews 6:4-6

to join us here in Ephesus soon, he's going to want to visit Rome as well. (There's no telling how soon he might be imprisoned again.)

Know that our brother Timothy has been released. If he comes soon, I will visit you with him. Greet all your leaders and all the disciples— those from Italy send their greetings.

Now for the final line:

Grace be with you all.

I threw down the reed, and leaned back in my chair. I sighed, then picked up the pages and jogged them together. Done. That was the moment I glanced at the left edge of my desk, and noticed another scroll that I had neglected completely: John's letter. Written to me personally, according to Milos. I picked it up, and walked over to the couch to make myself comfortable. Then I opened the letter and started reading.

The Elder, to the Chosen Lady—

The Chosen Lady. The address made me smile. So I read it again.

The Elder, to The Chosen Lady, and to her children.

There it was in writing. My children. I thought of all the years those two words filled my dreams. All the hopes, all the plans and expectations. So many nights I held them in my arms as I slept, and woke up barren again. I could even see their faces—as newborns, as infants, as toddlers, as young men and women. I saw them looking back at me—cooing, crying, laughing.

Calling me *Mama.*

No matter what they were going through, no matter the pain or the joy or the confusion, I would always be their mama. Not just to one or two—but to many. I was Avrah, mother of a multitude. Then my vision went dark, and I saw their faces. All of them. They passed before me, one by one. Young and old. Jewish and Greek. Slave and free.

I saw my children gathered around me in our courtyard, singing and praying and shouting into the rain. I saw my children learning Hebrew, learning to sew, learning to serve. I saw them feeding the hungry and clothing the naked in the Agora, in the Artemision, in the gutter. I saw my children.

My children. No cracked assemblage, or narcissist's forum, but a Body, whole and strong. A family with an eternal welcome. A home with doors that never shut.

The Elder, to the chosen lady and her children, whom I love in the truth—and not I alone, but also all who have come to know the truth—because of the truth that abides in us and will be with us forever: grace, mercy, and shalom be with us, from God the Father and from Messiah Jesus, the Father's Son, in truth and love!

I am overjoyed to find some of your children walking in truth, just as we received as a commandment from the Father. Now I ask you, dear lady, that we love one another. It is not as though I am writing you a new command, but the one we have had from the beginning. Now this is love: that we walk according to His commands. This is the commandment —just as you heard from the beginning—that you walk in love.

For many deceivers have gone out into the world—those who do not acknowledge Jesus as Messiah coming in human flesh. This one is a deceiver and the antichrist. Watch yourselves, so you do not lose what we have worked for but receive a full reward.

Anyone who goes too far and does not remain in Messiah's teaching does not have God. Anyone who remains in this teaching has both the Father and the Son. If anyone comes to you and does not bring this teaching, do not welcome him into your home or even give him a greeting. For the one greeting him shares in his evil deeds.

Forgiveness cannot always mean fellowship. ADONAI have mercy on his soul.

141

Although I have much to write to you, I don't want to do it with paper and ink. But I hope to return to you and speak face to face, so that our joy may be full.

Good. He's coming back soon.

The children of your Chosen Sister send you greetings.

My Chosen Sister. Hadassah. I messed them all so terribly. And yet, the comfort of this letter, and all that had happened this Pentecost, made the missing feel sweet. Almost like a gift.

In an impulse, I stood up from the couch and walked outside to sit on the bench in the courtyard. My eyes fell on the place where I'd buried the girl, expecting to see a mound of dirt next to the bench, and a stake with her name on it: *Avrah.* But it wasn't there.

I looked at the ground all around me. I was not myself at the time; perhaps I forgot where I buried her. I looked in every corner, behind every shrub and tree, every nook and cranny. But everywhere I looked, the grass was undisturbed. *I'm not crazy. John was there, too—he helped me!*

I plopped back down on the bench again, dumbfounded. I reached into my robe, and pulled out a lock of brown curly hair. I looked closer, and saw one strand that was not brown, but gray. *Whose hair is this?* My mind was spinning in circles, swirling in a tempest of puzzlement and self-doubt. But somehow my heart was able to drop anchor, and steady me with a fresh hope. A voice surfaced, from the depth of my being: *I will restore to you the years the locust has eaten. Then, you will eat and be satisfied.*[57]

I don't know how long I sat there in silence. But at some point Apollos came through the gate.

---

[57] Joel 2:25, 26

"Priscilla!" he greeted me brightly. "What are you doing?"

"Oh, I uh—" *I can't answer that.* "I was just looking for something. I'm fine." I tucked the hair back in my robe. "How are you? I didn't see you at Pentecost."

"I'm doing better, thanks. I was there, I just didn't feel like being seen. But what a day!" Apollos gripped his hair, as if he were at a loss for words. It's been a wild couple of days for Apollos. And a wild couple of weeks for all of us.

"I'm glad you didn't miss it," I smiled warmly. Then I took a risk. "How's Daphne?"

"I told her everything, Priscilla. I don't think I've ever apologized so much in my life."

"And?"

"And—she yelled at me. For about an hour. Then went silent for the next twenty-four. She just started talking to me again this afternoon."

I couldn't believe it. *More than a half-hour of silence from Daphne—* Apollos read the joke in my eyes.

"I know," he muttered. "It's a new record. But we're going to be fine. Maybe better than that. We want what you and Aquila have. A covenant-love."

"A covenant love," I repeated. "It began with a covenant, certainly. The sweetness came later. And went. And—came back again." I grinned. "It's there for you too."

"I never could have actually left her, Priscilla. Never."

"I know." I reached out and gripped his arm. "But I was worried anyway. And not just about you and Daphne." I stepped back and offered a reassuring smile. "Now, I assume you came for a reason?"

"Right, of course. I came to ask about your letter. The one to Rome?"

"Oh, yes!" I crossed the courtyard and went back inside to retrieve the letter into which I'd poured my entire being. I rolled the sheets together, then held my stamp to the candle flame, and sealed it shut. I put the translations of James and Jude in my robe, and returned to the courtyard.

"It is finished!" I declared, holding it before me ceremoniously, like an offering.

"Marvelous." Apollos laughed. He felt its weight in his hands. "I have no doubt that it's brilliant."

"More importantly—"

"Yes, I'm sure it's exactly what the Spirit has to say to the Hebrews in Rome."

"I hope so."

"Would you like me to take it to the harbor for you? The cargo ship to Rome is leaving in an hour. I promise not to board it myself." Apollos winked playfully, but I detected a note of sadness as well.

"If you don't mind." I pulled James and Jude out and handed them to Apollos as well. "These letters also need to go to Rome. Aquila just finished copying them so I can distribute them in Ephesus, too."

"James!" he exclaimed, glancing at the scrolls. "and Jude! I can't promise not to peek at these on my way to the harbor." He put a hand on my shoulder, and smiled warmly. "Well done, Mother Priscilla." I blushed, but he didn't see it. He'd already turned to leave the courtyard.

I stood and watched him walk through the gate, then returned to the sitting room and looked wistfully at my writing table. The salutation page was still there. I grabbed it from the table and rushed back out the door, out the gate and onto the street. Apollos was already several doors away.

"Apollos! Wait!" I shouted. He turned around with an inquisitive look, and I jogged down the hill toward him. "I forgot the salutation!"

"It's fine!" he shouted back. "You already sealed it."

"But—" I panted. "How will they know it's from me?"

"Trust me," Apollos winked, before turning back toward the harbor. "They'll know."

THE TEACHING

Commentary on the Story

Note: This section is intended as a reference. The notes herein may be read sequentially, or simply referred to as needed. Characterizations and plot points described in this section are believed by the authors to be feasible and realistic. However, they are not specifically supported by historical evidence, unless otherwise indicated.

The Characters

I Am Priscilla features a blend of characters which are based on a combination of knowable historical facts from Scripture, and on the imaginations of the authors. The objective is to draw as much insight as possible from biblical sources, before filling in the gaps with historical research, educated guesses, and poetic license. Some additional characters, such as Hadassah or Milos, are invented for narrative purposes.

The following profiles are provided for those characters in the story which are based directly on people mentioned in Scripture.

Priscilla

Although Priscilla is only mentioned six times in Scripture, it is enough to gather that she was a preeminent teacher of the first-century church. Drawing strictly from Scripture, we can know the following facts about Priscilla:

She lived, at one point, in Rome with her husband Aquila, who was a Jewish man from Pontus, in Asia minor. They were both expelled from Italy by the Emperor Claudius.

She and Aquila are always mentioned together, and in four of the six instances, Priscilla is mentioned first. (This runs counter to the cultural practice, suggesting that Priscilla was the more prominent member of the pair.) *Note: All the remaining facts about Priscilla are equally true of Aquila.*

Priscilla met Paul in Corinth, then sailed with him to Ephesus. (Paul's final destination was Syria, but he spent well over a year in Ephesus with the couple, on the way.)

Paul refers to Priscilla as his "fellow worker" in writing his letter to the Romans. She would have been living in Rome at the time that city received Paul's letter.

Priscilla and Aquila would have been with Paul in Asia Minor (almost certainly Ephesus), at the time of the writing of his first letter to the Corinthians, in order for him to greet, on their behalf, the church in Corinth, which met in what used to be their house.

Priscilla would have been living in the same city as Timothy when he received Paul's second letter. (Again, this is almost certainly Ephesus.)

Though these facts are fascinating, they're hardly enough to build a story around. However, there is one additional assumption, grounded in serious biblical research, which adds an enormous resource to the authors' historical and scriptural toolbox. That assumption is this: Priscilla was the author of the biblical epistle to the Hebrews. Read more about this assumption on page 157. For the purposes of this profile, however, the questions below are based on the premise that Priscilla was indeed the author of Hebrews.

Was Priscilla Jewish? If Priscilla was indeed the author of the epistle to the Hebrews, it seems a stretch to conclude that she was not herself Jewish. Her presumed authority amongst a group of Jewish Believers, and her deep knowledge of the Hebrew Scriptures and Temple system should be evidence enough. The bigger question, then, is in regard to her country of origin.

Where was she born and raised? There is compelling archaeological evidence that Priscilla had family roots in Rome, and strong connections to Roman society. Therefore, some scholars conclude that she was a Roman national, and a convert to Christianity, and possibly also to Judaism. This may be the easiest solution, albeit not the one chosen for the sake of this story. In the opinion of the authors, it strengthens Priscilla's position to have originated in the land of Israel. It also improves her likelihood to have been an eyewitness of Jesus' ministry. Which brings us to the next question:

Was she an eyewitness, or even a follower, of Jesus during his earthly ministry? Most scholars would conclude that the author of Hebrews was not, based on Hebrews 2:3b: "It was first spoken through the Lord and confirmed to us by those who heard." This phrasing puts the odds against the author having experienced Jesus' ministry directly. However, it does not rule it out, since the word "confirmed" leaves the door open for other eyewitnesses to bolster the author's own first-hand observation of Jesus' ministry. There is no room for dogma here, but for the sake of this story, the authors have chosen to make Priscilla an eyewitness, a follower, and even a financial supporter of Jesus during his time on earth.

As a woman, could Priscilla have been a leader in the first-century church? Customs have varied wildly throughout the history of the church, as have interpretations of Scripture, regarding the appropriate opportunities for female leadership. Nevertheless, it is clear from a plain and holistic reading of Paul's letters that he regarded certain women as "partners" in ministry, deserving of high esteem. Of these, Priscilla is perhaps the most prominent, since she is regularly named before her husband. She is also credited with having taught Apollos (a rising pillar in the church) and risking her life to save that of Paul. Thus, even those who view the role of Pastor as inappropriate for a woman must consider the role of Prophetess, as evidenced by Joel 2:28, Acts 21:9 and I Corinthians 11:5.

This story takes full advantage of Priscilla's qualifications as a prophetess, and an influencer of the early church, but refrains from making her the sole (or "lead") pastor of any discrete group of Believers. This is done in order to keep the focus where it belongs, instead of sparking a debate about the role of women in the church.

When was she born? Did she have children? There are no apparent theories among scholars to answer this question one way or another. The authors have chosen here to make Priscilla fifty-two years old at the time of the story, and also barren, as a means of developing her journey as a character.

Aquila

As stated above, Aquila is historically never mentioned apart from Priscilla. However, the authors do make certain unique assumptions about Aquila, for the sake of the narrative, as follows:

Aquila settled in Rome before meeting Priscilla in Jerusalem. This plot point involves Aquila being one of the original Believers, and also gives Priscilla a reason to relocate from Israel to Rome, after agreeing to marry Aquila.

Aquila was a proficient teacher and respected leader. Although Priscilla receives top billing, Aquila is not excluded from Paul's accolades, and should receive credit as a fellow hero of the early church.

Aquila's marriage to Priscilla was uneasy. The preeminence of a wife over a husband is a potential source of disharmony even in modern marriages, not to mention those of the Ancient Near East. In this edition, the challenges of such a marriage form the backdrop of Aquila's relationship with Priscilla. Future editions may develop this dynamic further.

John the Apostle

John son of Zebedee (John the Apostle, John the Beloved, John the Evangelist) was one of the twelve disciples appointed by Jesus. Among the twelve were the sons of Zebedee—John and his older brother James— whom Jesus called "Sons of Thunder". This John should not be confused with John the Baptist (John the Baptizer, John the Immerser) who was Jesus' cousin.

John, being the youngest of the disciples, may have been just thirteen years old at the beginning of Jesus' ministry, and in his late forties at the time of this story. Thus, even though it is implied that his preferred title for himself is "The Elder" he would have been a few years younger than our fictional version of Priscilla.

The plot of this story depends, in part, on the past role of John in caring for Jesus' mother Mary. Many have concluded that he relocated from Israel to Ephesus early in his ministry, and brought Mary with him, eventually building her a house on Mt. Koressos, immediately south of the city. John ministers both locally and abroad, as the Spirit leads him. As such, he does not hold a distinct office within any given local church, and handles his outsized influence with light touch.

John authored five books of the New Testament: the Gospel of John, the three epistles commonly known as I John, II John and III John, and the book of Revelation. For more about II John, see page 158.

Apollos

Apollos receives a number of mentions in the book of Acts and Paul's letters, but almost nothing is offered by way of biography. All we know from Scripture is that he was a Jewish man from Alexandria, that he traveled in Paul's circle, ministering in Corinth and Ephesus, and that he became so influential within the faith that his name at one time appeared alongside (and perhaps in contrast to) those of Paul and Peter.

One final fact that can be gleaned from Scripture is that, prior to his period of influence Apollos had a teaching ministry, wherein he was only acquainted with the "baptism of John". This baptism likely refers to Jewish immersion for repentance and ritual cleanliness, without regard to Jesus' commandment to baptize in the name of the Father, the Son and the Holy Spirit. At a later point, Priscilla and Aquila took Apollos aside to "teach him the way of God more accurately," as Paul put it.

A number of theories exist about this "conversion" story, involving some scholarly disagreement about whether Apollos was indeed a Believer (Christian) prior to his tutelage with Priscilla and Aquila. For the purposes of this story, the idea of being only acquainted with the baptism of John strongly implies that Apollos' theology and worldview are pre-Messianic. Thus, his encounter with Priscilla and Aquila was needed to bring him fully into the family of Jesus, even though he was already well-versed in the facts about the Messiah.

The authors have presumed that Apollos had a very successful teaching ministry, and that he was so revered for his storytelling that he was reluctant to change anything, least of all to surrender his heart to a Savior. This is why Priscilla and Aquila were so instrumental in his life and future ministry.

Nicolas / Nicolaitans

Although the person of Nicolas appears in Scripture only tangentially, his work is mentioned explicitly in several places. The clearest example is in the second chapter of the book of Revelation. In that chapter, Jesus, as recorded by John the Apostle, commends the Believers in Ephesus for rejecting the way of the Nicolaitans, and warns the Believers in Pergamum because some of them do follow those teachings.

Very little could be drawn from these two references, if not for the writings of multiple early church fathers, who cite Nicolas, Deacon of Jerusalem, as the namesake of the heretical faction. Some scholars note the juxtaposition of the Nicolaitans with Balaam in Revelation, to characterize the teachings of Nicolas as a rejection of all moral standards, resulting in idol worship and sexual immorality. This philosophy is often referred to as antinomianism.

If this interpretation of the Nicolaitans is accurate, it becomes visible all throughout the writings of the New Testament (and even the Gospel of John), as the writers struggle to refute the idea that Jesus' work on the cross has freed his followers from the very concept of obedience.

As for the character Nicolas, the sixth chapter of Acts names him as one of the seven original deacons in Jerusalem. The premise here supposes a downward slide over the three decades between his appointment and the events of this story. By the time he meets Priscilla, Nicolas—being an intensely charming and persuasive individual—has become highly influential and fully committed to his wayward path. By this point in his life, everyone he meets is either an adversary, or a tool for his own agenda.

Other Characters

Paul the Apostle. Although they consider one another partners in ministry, Paul and Priscilla's face-to-face relationship, by this point, is mostly in the past. Nevertheless, the receipt of Paul's letter to the Ephesians toward the end of the story gives Paul a powerful voice in the story's outcome.

Peter the Apostle. Peter was very influential in Priscilla's life in Rome for a few years. It is probable that Peter's first (and perhaps only) visit to Rome in AD 42 may have provided the spark that caused the believing community and that city to achieve its first real period of growth. Peter is not a character in this story, but is mentioned by Priscilla as an important person in her journey.

Gaius. Gaius is a member of an elite circle of Christians (including Priscilla, Aquila, Paul and Apollos) who gained notoriety in both Corinth and Ephesus. He was one of the few people Paul admits to having baptized personally, and he traveled extensively with Paul on his missionary journeys. As a consequence, Gaius (along with Aristarchus) was violently targeted by the rioting crowd in Ephesus (Acts 19) but was ultimately unharmed. Gaius' name appears again as the recipient of the third letter of John, implying that he is a leader of the Believers in Ephesus. It is presumed that III John is written a few years after the events of this story, wherein Gaius is presented as the primary leader of the city-wide church.

Diotrephes. Another leader mentioned in the letter of III John is Diotrephes, who is characterized as someone who "always wants to be first." The story puts him in a secondary position to Gaius—trusted, but cautiously. His ego is suspect, which makes him susceptible to the influence of Nicolas. This becomes especially problematic when Diotrephes has the opportunity to attain sole leadership of the city-wide community of believers.

Demetrius. The name Demetrius appears twice in the New Testament—once as the instigator of the aforementioned Ephesian riot, and a second time in III John, wherein he receives accolades from the Elder. It is by no means certain that these two are actually one in the same person, especially since one acts as an enemy of the faith, and the other is a trusted member of it. However, this story presumes them to be one and the same.

The Setting

Jerusalem / Capernaum

As the story begins, Jerusalem is in a state of pandemonium. This is a probable scenario during the festival of Passover at this time in history. Priscilla begins the story by recounting the martyrdom of James which occurs here (according to the historical record) and is covered in the first book of the trilogy.

On her way from Jerusalem to the port of Ptolemais, she and her traveling party stop in Capernaum, on the Sea of Galilee. This site was chosen for the story because of its significance in the Gospels, and its reputation as a regional center for rabbinical education. Thus, it is a fitting point of origin for Priscilla and her fictional sister Hadassah, each of whom becomes known for her first-rate intellect.

Mediterranean Sea / Aegean Sea

Priscilla's life, such as it is known, was characterized by sea travel.

This is evidenced in part by her use of the word "anchor" as a spiritual metaphor (Hebrews 6:19 – the only such example in Scripture.) The journey depicted here is fraught with troubles which were common amongst crossings of the Mediterranean. (See "Natural Disasters" below.)

Ephesus / Ephesian Church

The bulk of the story takes places in the ancient city of Ephesus. After Rome, Ephesus was arguably the "second city" of the first-century Roman Empire, as well as the undisputed commercial capital, and largest city, in Asia Minor (modern-day Turkey).

At the time of this story, the city of Ephesus was enjoying its golden age. It housed between a quarter and half a million residents, and boasted the largest temple—the Temple of Artemis—that the ancient world had ever known. It also featured an enormous amphitheater, which was cut into the side of Mount Pion facing the Harbor, which was famous for seating up to 25,000 people on its steep risers.

Ephesus was an extremely progressive and diverse city. Any stroll down the Arcadian Way (from the harbor to the theatre) or Curetes Way (from the theatre to the agoras and the far eastern wall) would introduce the visitor to a cross-section of the entire Roman empire—soldiers and slaves, aristocrats and beggars, pagans, Jews and Christians. Women (like Priscilla) enjoyed comparative privilege, regularly owning land or businesses, and even serving in some minor positions of leadership.

To the south of the city rose Mt. Koressos, where it is presumed that John the Apostle constructed a house for Mary the mother of Jesus, to give her refuge from the noise and chaos of urbanity. A house remains there to this day to bolster that claim, hosting visitors from every corner of the globe. John's own house is said to sit in the hills above and behind the Temple of Artemis.

Another famous event in Ephesus was the great riot at the Theatre, recorded in chapter 19 of the book of Acts. This episode highlights the intense pride and loyalty of Ephesians for their patron goddess Artemis, and the challenges posed thereby for Christians in the city.

Ephesus, at its core, was a port city, and its commercial success depended almost entirely upon sea traffic from the Bay of Ephesus off the Aegean Sea. Although it was perfectly situated to ship grain and other products from inland Asia Minor to the Greco-Roman world, and to serve as a waystation for busy routes, Ephesus had a major problem. The nearby Cayster River emptied into the Bay of Ephesus immediately to the north of the city, dumping enormous quantities of silt into the bay. This silt threatened to block vessels from entering the city's harbor. Over the centuries, an artificial harbor was built, along with a shipping channel to reach it, which was lengthened again and again as the issue worsened. Ultimately, it became so difficult and expensive to bring ships into the harbor that the effort was abandoned. Not long thereafter the city shrank, then died, then faded into the pile of ruins we see today.

Despite their minority status, Believers in Jesus had a strong presence in the city by the time of this story. Although the Ephesian Believers' precise customs of assembly and administration are unknown, the authors have presumed that it functioned as a network of house churches. Each house church would meet, naturally, in a private home, and be led by its own pastor, elder, or small group of trusted individuals. These leaders, in turn, would be accountable to an overseer, and perhaps to a group of elders, like a modern-day board of directors. For the purposes of this story, Gaius holds the position as the sole head of the Ephesian church, with Diotrephes serving as his deputy.

Natural Disasters

The story of Priscilla is driven, in part, by the natural disasters she experiences, both directly and indirectly. In particular, the storm the characters endure on their sea voyage is consistent with one recorded by Tacitus, which destroyed 200 ships harbored at Naples in the year AD 62. It is presumed that Italy received the most direct hit from the storm, and that faraway ships such as Priscilla's, in the eastern Mediterranean, might have been able to drop anchor and escape with minimal damage.

More central to the plot is the occurrence of multiple earthquakes known to have hit Southern Europe during the years AD 60-63. The areas known to have suffered the greatest impact are Campania (Italy), Macedonia and Achaea (Greece), and western Phrygia (Asia Minor). Notable cities in Phrygia to have been affected are Colossae and Laodicea, both of which boasted historically significant communities of Believers. Mostly recorded by the historian Tacitus, there is some debate among scholars regarding the timing of these tremors, and even whether some of them represented the same exact event, spread across a vast region.

Lastly, a reference is made to a tsunami which devastates the nation of Cyprus. While there is no historical record of such an event, it is reasonable to suppose that an earthquake centered at Colossae would have a ripple effect on the waters of the Mediterranean, which would in turn endanger the nearby island of Cyprus and its low-lying population.

Epistles in the Narrative

Hebrews

As mentioned above, the story presumes Priscilla to have been the author of the Letter to the Hebrews, written to an audience of Jewish Believers living in Rome.

The case for her authorship has been laid out in grand detail in the book *Priscilla's Letter,* by Ruth Hoppin. Thus, there is no need to repeat it here. Suffice it to say that none of the candidates (all male) put forward for authorship throughout history would have had any reason for their names to be suppressed from the work. But Priscilla's gender, on the other hand, may very well have prevented the letter from gaining universal acceptance, thereby justifying its early distributors in anonymizing it.

In the story, Priscilla writes the letter in response to one she receives from that community, which paints a dark picture of its spiritual state.

She struggles to work out exactly what to tell them, and as she does so, begins to see the same issues manifesting themselves in her own community in Ephesus. The final result of her work is revealed in the book of Hebrews as it appears in the canon of Scripture.

Ephesians

Since most of the story takes place in the city of Ephesus, and since Paul's epistle to that city is likely to have been received around the time the story is set (AD 62) the letter plays a plausible role the narrative. This story is designed, in part, to reverse-engineer Paul's message in Ephesians, and imagine what sort of issues might have motivated his precise message. For example, a cursory reading of Ephesians conveys that the original intended audience needed a lot of encouragement to worship in unity, which is a key feature of the celebration of Pentecost. Thus the two are linked for the sake of the narrative.

II John

Wholly apart from the question of the authorship of Hebrews, some scholars have theorized that John's second letter was addressed to Priscilla personally, referring to her as "the Chosen [or Elect] Lady." The story presumes that her "children", to whom John refers, are her many spiritual sons and daughters. It also addresses the issue of a false prophet, or group of false prophets, which is presumed in the narrative to refer directly to Nicolas and the Nicolaitans. This is especially plausible if one credits the writing of Revelation (in which the Nicolaitans are denounced by name, not once, but twice) to the same John.

The Festivals

To be a Christian, by definition, is to be a "little Christ". To be like Jesus. This is what Jesus means when he calls us to be disciples, and to make disciples. A genuine Christians is a person who strives to walk, talk, think and act just like Jesus would, if he were in our shoes.

The New Testament is the divinely inspired guide for all those who aspire to discipleship. The Gospels tell us the story of Jesus' ministry, death, resurrection and ascension. The Acts of the Apostles recounts the story of Pentecost and the early years of the Church. And the Epistles explain in greater detail what these stories mean for us, and how to make the kinds of choices in our lives that Jesus might make.

However, the New Testament is only a portion of what God has given us to understand the life of a disciple. After all, Jesus didn't have any of it. He read and studied and lived by the Hebrew Scriptures—the Law of Moses, the Prophets, and the Writings.[58] The writers of the New Testament were all, or nearly all, Jewish like Jesus. And if there is any doubt about the importance of the Old Testament in understanding the New, note that the latter quotes the former over 800 times. If one were to include indirect quotations and allusions the number would be in the thousands. In short, the entire New Testament is drawn from the concepts, prophecies and history of the Old.

One major example of the patterns of the Old Testament providing a framework for the New is that of the Jewish Festivals, especially the seven Levitical Festivals outlined in Leviticus 23.

---

[58] Or, in Hebrew: *Torah, Nevi'im, Ketuvim,* the abbreviation of which produces the name of the Jewish equivalent to the Old Testament: *The Tanakh.*

The festivals provide a yearly life cycle which also affects the way practitioners live on a daily basis. It is a way of living that reminds us never to forget our salvation and the goodness of God. As the Lord instructs us in Deuteronomy 6:10-12: "When the Lord your God brings you into the land he swore to your fathers ... then when you eat and are satisfied, *be careful that you do not forget the Lord,* who brought you out of Egypt, out of the land of slavery."

When we are grounded in our historical Biblical roots, not only by our knowledge but also but our pattern of living and as a way of life it helps to preserve us so that we do not forget. In celebrating Resurrection Sunday it takes us back to the resurrection of Jesus but we must not stop there, for the resurrection is rooted in Passover. We must continue back to the foundation of Resurrection Sunday which is our Abrahamic roots and the covenant God made with him. As Paul says "Abraham is the father of all that believe." [59] We must not forget our historical roots lest we drift astray.

The Seven Levitical Festivals

The Lord said to Moses, "Speak to the Israelites and say to them 'These are my appointed feasts, the appointed feasts of the Lord, which you are to proclaim as sacred assemblies.'" [60]

The Seven Levitical Festivals are found in Exodus, Leviticus, Numbers and Deuteronomy but Leviticus 23 serves well as a primary source. As verse four proclaims, "These are the Lord's appointed feasts, the sacred assemblies you are to proclaim at their times." They do not belong to any group of humans, or to humanity in general. Instead, they belong to God. And we are called to enter into them as we proclaim them to the world.

Even some who are conversant with the Jewish calendar may be unfamiliar with a few of the festivals listed below. This is because the

---

[59] Romans 4:11
[60] Leviticus 23:1-2

Passover is conventionally viewed and celebrated as a single eight-day festival, but in the Torah it is outlined as three distinct times: Passover (one day), Unleavened Bread (the following seven days), and First Fruits (one day, within the seven days of Unleavened Bread). Furthermore, some of the more popular holidays, such as Hanukkah and Purim, were instituted after the Torah was written.

Below is a brief overview of the original Seven Levitical Festivals. Further detail on Passover and the Feast of Weeks (Shavu'ot) is provided in a later section.

Passover (Pesach) and the New Year

"The Lord's Passover begins at twilight on the fourteenth day of the first month." [61]

The biblical new year starts in the spring as commanded by God in Exodus 12:2, "This month is to be for you the first month … of your year." None of the months had names at this point. (Today Judaism calls the first month Nisan.) Passover [62] begins on the fifteenth day of the first month.

The importance of this cannot be overstated. In Joshua, the Lord had the Israelites enter the Promised Land at the start of the new year. In fact the first thing that the Israelites did once in the land, after crossing the Jordan and setting up the twelve standing stones, was to celebrate the Passover. [63]

Passover was also important to Mary and Joseph, the parents of Jesus. Luke 2:41 records that, "Every year [Jesus'] parents went to Jerusalem for the Feast of Passover." It was only a requirement that Joseph go but since both of his parents went it would be reasonable to assume that they took

---

[61] Leviticus 23:5

[62] *Pesach* in Hebrew which means "to spring, jump or pass over" something.

[63] Joshua 4:19-5:15

the children and travelled with many friends and relatives.[64] Jesus probably celebrated Passover in Jerusalem all of his adult life and many of his childhood years. He also stated that he eagerly desired[65] to celebrate the Passover with his disciples.[66]

Aside from the Gospels, allusions to Passover are found all throughout the New Testament. The book of Revelation, for example, contains many references to the Exodus-Passover event when referring to the Song of Moses and in referring to Jesus as the Lamb.

Unleavened Bread (Matzah)

"On the fifteenth day of that month the Lord's Feast of Unleavened Bread begins; for seven days you must eat bread made without yeast." [67]

The feast of unleavened bread begins on the day after Passover and lasts for seven days – from the evening of the sixteenth day until the evening of the twenty-second day. Biblically, Passover and Unleavened Bread are two separate festivals but are commonly called the eight days of Passover in Judaism today.

The time of Unleavened Bread is fairly self-explanatory, as it is focused on the avoidance of leaven, or yeast, in the household. This is the reason for the ritual eating of *matzah,* or unleavened bread. Multiple references to this in the New Testament use yeast as a metaphor for sin. This is especially significant when Jesus compares the *matzah* to his own body, which is "broken" for us. Just as there was no yeast in the bread, there was no sin in his body.

First Fruits (Yom HaBikkurim)

"Speak to the Israelites and say to them: 'When you enter the land I am going to give you and you reap its harvest, bring to the priest a sheaf

---

[64] Joachim, Jeremias, Jerusalem in the Time of Jesus
[65] Luke 22:15
[66] Luke 22:7-22, Matthew 26:17-30, Mark 14:12-26, John 13:1-30
[67] Leviticus 23:6

of the first grain you harvest. He is to wave the sheaf before the Lord so it will be accepted on your behalf; the priest is to wave it on the day after the Sabbath." [68]

The feast of First Fruits begins the day after the Passover Sabbath. The Pharisees, and later Rabbinic Judaism, interpreted this to mean the day after Passover (the first day of Unleavened Bread), but the Sadducees and others believed it occurred on the day after the regular Sabbath during or after Passover. The latter interpretation causes First Fruits to always fall on the Sunday within the eight days of Passover/Unleavened bread.

This is important because Sunday, or the first day of the week, signifies new beginnings and relates to the number eight as a number of dedication. As we will see further down, this interpretation also causes Shavu'ot to always fall on a Sunday.

Feast of Weeks (Shavu'ot / Pentecost)

"From the day after the Sabbath the day you brought the sheaf of the wave offering, count off seven full weeks. Count off fifty days up to the day after the seventh Sabbath and then present an offering of new grain to the Lord." [69]

After the festival of First Fruits comes the counting of the fifty days, called the Counting of the Omer (explained in more detail in a later section) which leads up to the festival of Shavu'ot. This festival is also known as the "latter first fruits" because the fruit of the wheat harvest was brought in and waved before the Lord in worship and thanksgiving. Barney Kasdan, a Messianic Jewish Rabbi, writes in his excellent book, *God's Appointed Times*: "Shavu'ot is designated as a time of thanksgiving for the early harvest. God's faithfulness in providing the early wheat harvest increases hopefulness for an abundant fall harvest (at Sukkot). [70]

Also known as Pentecost, this festival is related to the giving of the

---

[68] Leviticus 23:10-11
[69] Leviticus 23:15-16
[70] Kasdan, 52.

law to Moses at Mt. Sinai in the third month. [71] It takes place in the third month of the Jewish calendar, which is known as Sivan and starts in late May or early June. Since Shavu'ot, or Pentecost, is the primary focus of this book, it is described in much greater detail in other sections.

Feast of Trumpets (Rosh Hashanah / Yom Teruah)

"On the first day of the seventh month you are to have a day of rest, a sacred assembly commemorated with trumpet blasts. Do no regular work but present an offering made to the Lord by fire." [72]

The Feast of Trumpets celebrates the Jewish civil new year and should not be confused with the biblical new year that starts in the Spring. Scripture is brief on the subject, but establishes the Feast of Trumpets as a time of regathering, initiating the ten days of preparation for the Day of Atonement. The trumpet blasts are considered the "wake-up call; an alarm to call us to our appointed time." [73]

Day of Atonement (Yom Kippur)

"The tenth day of this seventh month is the Day of Atonement. Hold a sacred assembly and deny yourselves, and present an offering made to the Lord by fire. Do no work on that day, because it is the Day of Atonement, when atonement is made for you before the Lord your God. Anyone who does not deny himself on that day must be cut off from his people. I will destroy from among his people anyone who does any work on that day. You shall do no work at all. This is to be a lasting ordinance for the generations to come, wherever you live. It is a sabbath of rest for you, and you must deny yourselves. From the evening of the ninth day of the month until the following evening you are to observe your sabbath." [74]

---

[71] Exodus 19:1
[72] Leviticus 23:23-25
[73] Kasdan, 65.
[74] Leviticus 23:26-32

The Day of Atonement is considered the holiest day of the year with all thirty-four verses of Leviticus chapter sixteen being devoted to the explicit way in which it was to be observed. This was the day when the high priest would enter the Holy of Holies to make "atonement for himself, his household and the whole community of Israel." [75]

Kasdan writes: "Yom Kippur is considered the logical extension of what was started at Rosh Hashanah. In fact, the ten days between Rosh Hashanah and Yom Kippur take on their own holy significance. They're called the Yomim Nora'im, The Days of Awe. Traditional Jews, as well as many non-traditional Jews, spend these days looking inward, seeing how their inner life might be more pleasing to God. Personal relationships are evaluated; forgiveness and restitution are offered where needed. Reconciliation is attempted." [76]

Feast of Tabernacles (Sukkot)

"The Lord said to Moses, 'Say to the Israelites: "On the fifteenth day of the seventh month the Lord's Feast of Tabernacles begins, and it lasts for seven days. The first day is a sacred assembly; do no regular work. For seven days present offerings made to the Lord by fire, and on the eighth day hold a sacred assembly and present an offering made to the Lord by fire. It is the closing assembly; do no regular work."'" [77]

The Feast Tabernacles is the last of the festivals and as such sums up all of the previous six. The festival year that began with Passover is now concluded with Sukkot. It is very special because it is the *seventh* festival, it begins in the *seventh* month, and lasts for *seven* days. It is a time for thanksgiving and celebration—a time, as Nehemiah said, to "enjoy choice food and sweet drink, and send some to those who have nothing prepared. This day is sacred to our Lord. Do not grieve, for the joy of the

---

[75] Leviticus 16:17
[76] Kasdan, 79
[77] Leviticus 23:33-36

Lord is your strength." [78] The Feast of Tabernacles also has a strong future aspect. Zechariah foretells a day when all nations will stream to Jerusalem to celebrate the Festival, and Revelation chapter 19 reveals its ultimate fulfillment in the Marriage Supper of the Lamb.

Past, Present and Future

All the festivals have a past, a present and a future aspect to them. They were given in the past as outworkings of the covenant relationship between God and Israel. They are a present reality in our yearly community life cycle as well as our daily lives. and they all will have a future fulfillment in the Kingdom of God.

Dan Juster, a Messianic Jewish Rabbi and noted scholar writes: "I have come to see all the feasts as having great future prophetic reference awaiting fulfillment. Hence each feast has historic reference to God's salvation to ancient Israel, to the meaning of fulfillment in Yeshua [Jesus] who brings out the deepest meaning of the feast, to agricultural significance in celebrating God as the provider, and reference to the last days and the millennial age to come. [79]

The Spirit and the Festivals

This book demonstrates the centrality of Shavu'ot / Pentecost to the plan of God, and specifically to the great outpouring of the Holy Spirit in Jerusalem after Jesus' ascension. But Shavu'ot is not the only festival which reveals the character of the Spirit of God. Like the Holy Spirit (as revealed at the Great Outpouring) the Seven Levitical Festivals are (1) Experiential, (2) Integrated, (3) Communal and (4) Evangelistic.

Experiential. The festivals are not services but feast days to be lived. These commands are to be an integral part of the community life of Israel, as well as individual and family life. They are to be impressed

---

[78] Nehemiah 8:10
[79] Juster, *Jewish Roots,* viii

(taught) to the children, to be passed down throughout the generations. It is the responsibility of parents to observe and teach these truths. Likewise, baptism in the Holy Spirit is evidenced by the *experience* of speaking in tongues and praising God.

Integrated. The festivals are integrated because the observance of each festival is not a performance or entertainment oriented that is put on by a leader and choir. Likewise, the work of the Holy Spirit comes to the entire group at once, and not through the leadership of an individual.

Communal. The festivals are communal because all of the family and community observe them. Likewise, the Great Outpouring was a communal event that drew no lines of separation between different groups of people. To the contrary, it eliminated the dividing lines, much like the curtain in the Agora, in Priscilla's story.

Evangelistic. The festivals are evangelistic because of the opportunity to invite the foreigner and alien to participate in them. Likewise, the Holy Spirit worked in the hearts of the crowd on the day of Pentecost, and about three thousand of them became Believers.

Passover and the Pilgrimage Festivals

Of the seven feasts, three of them, Passover, Shavu'ot (Pentecost) and Sukkot (Tabernacles) are called Pilgrimage Festivals because they required all the men in the land of Israel to appear before the Lord. [80] The Pilgrimage Festivals form the basis for this trilogy, as the three books feature these three festivals, respectively. In this section, they are discussed through the lens of Passover, as the primary festival.

The first appointed time is Passover, which first defined Israel as a nation in Exodus chapter 12. The command to celebrate Passover and begin the New Year with this observance was the first command given to the children of Israel. Thus their calling, mission and identity are bound

---

[80] Exodus 23:17, 34:23, Deuteronomy 16:16

up in Passover and the Passover-Exodus event.

Passover is the primary festival because it initiates the festival season and lends significance to all seven festivals. Further, it is an essential component of the three Pilgrimage Festivals. The Passover-Shavu'ot relationship is particularly strong because it is connected by the Counting of the Omer (the 50 days) and the journey from Exodus to Mt. Sinai. Thus Shavu'ot is called the *atzeret,* or "conclusion" of Passover. The journey that began in Egypt in the first month of the year brought the Israelites to Mt. Sinai in the third month.

This same relationship exists between Passover and Sukkot (The Feast of Tabernacles). In essence Sukkot draws its identity from Passover as well as from Shavu'ot, and fulfills and completes both of them. The three Pilgrimage Festivals are thus integral to one another and could be compared to the triune nature and revelation of the Godhead: the Son (Passover), the Spirit (Pentecost) and the Father (Tabernacles).

The centrality of Passover to the three Pilgrimage Festivals, the seven Levitical festivals, and indeed, to the redemptive master story of God in both the Old and New Testaments, is the rationale for naming this series The Passover Trilogy. While the second book is primarily about Pentecost, and the third book is primarily about the Feast of Tabernacles, these are rooted in, and surrounded by, the redemptive master-themes of Passover.

Counting of the Omer

As described in the Introduction, Passover marks the barley harvest in mid-Spring, and begins the countdown to the wheat harvest in late Spring. In Leviticus 23:15, God commands "Then you are to count from the day after the Sabbath, from the day that you brought the Omer [a unit of measure] of the wave offering, seven complete Sabbaths. Until the day after the seventh Sabbath you are to count fifty days, and then present a new grain offering to ADONAI."

This new grain offering marks the festival of Shavu'ot, or Pentecost. Thus, for thousands of years Jewish people have counted fifty days from Passover to Pentecost, which is referred to as the Counting of the Omer.

Shavu'ot (Feast of Weeks)

As explained in the Introduction, Shavu'ot is one of the seven holidays prescribed in Leviticus 23 for Israel to observe in perpetuity. At its root, Shavu'ot is a celebration of the wheat harvest, which comes seven weeks, or fifty days, after the barley harvest, represented by the festivals of Passover and First Fruits.

While Passover[81] calls forth the children of Israel from bondage in Egypt, Shavu'ot[82] is the time when Israel was called as a nation into a covenantal relationship with God, through the giving of the Law to Moses on Mt. Sinai. Shavu'ot/Pentecost then provided the way of fulfilling that calling by bringing the righteousness and justice of the Kingdom of God to the earth (to all nations).

It was supposed that the Children of Israel had arrived at Sinai on the fiftieth day after their Exodus from Egypt, thus adding a new layer of meaning to the festival. With this, what had begun as an agricultural observance became something much richer and deeper. This association—between Shavu'ot and the giving of the Law—set the stage for the Great Outpouring of the Holy Spirit among Jewish followers of Jesus, as told in the second chapter of the book of Acts.

Of the three pilgrimage festivals, Shavu'ot may receive the least attention, as it tends to be overshadowed by Passover and Sukkot (Tabernacles). Its one-day observance is brief in comparison to the eight days of Passover/Unleavened Bread and the seven/eight days of Sukkot. And, whereas Passover is celebrated with a grand Seder (meal) and Sukkot with the building of a sukkah (tent or booth), Shavu'ot's lack of

---

[81] Exodus 12
[82] Exodus 19:1

169

memorable liturgy or communal activity can make it seem forgettable. However, the significance of Shavu'ot in the establishment of a national covenant is central to the plan of God, in fulfilling the covenantal promises he made to Abraham and, by extension, to every nation. [83]

This theme of Mission, starting with the promise and blessing of Abraham and reaching around the world, is reflected clearly in Psalm 67, which is a core element of the celebration of Shavu'ot. The key phrase is in verse 2, "that your ways may be known on earth, your salvation among all the nations." What began as an agricultural harvest-festival blossoms in this way into an eschatological harvest of souls from every corner of the world.

Thus, while Shavu'ot is not the most well-known of Jewish holidays, it continues to occupy an important place on the Hebrew calendar. It is viewed by many Jews as the culmination of Passover, just as the receiving of the Torah on Mount Sinai was the culmination of the Exodus from Egypt.

This is why Jewish people celebrate Shavu'ot with activities and liturgies that commemorate the inception of the Law of Moses, and why it is a popular time for confirmation and rededication to Jewish practice and the study of that Law. It is also common to eat dairy foods and other sweet foods, and to read the book of Ruth as a congregation.

When is Shavu'ot?

There are two perspectives on the timing of Shavu'ot. One perspective begins the Counting of the Omer on the second day of Passover. This causes Shavu'ot to always fall on the sixth day of Sivan, which is the third month, regardless of what day of the week it is. As explained above, this is exactly fifty days (or seven weeks plus one day) after Passover, which falls on the fifteenth day of Nisan.

Another perspective begins the Counting of the Omer on the first Sabbath during Passover, causing Shavu'ot to always fall on a Sunday,

---

[83] See *JPS Torah Commentary: Exodus*, "The Covenant at Sinai", 102.

regardless of the date. This is the perspective which was more or less adopted by Church tradition, since Pentecost always falls on a Sunday.

Due to the lunisolar nature of the Jewish calendar, compared to the strictly solar Gregorian calendar, Shavu'ot and Pentecost are sometimes perfectly aligned, and sometimes up to four weeks apart. Regardless of the perspective to which one prescribes, Shavu'ot will always fall somewhere between mid-May and mid-June.

Pentecost

The Christian Church celebrates Pentecost with a heavy emphasis on the specific event which took place in Jerusalem on Shavu'ot, fifty days after the crucifixion of Jesus (approx. AD 30). Geza Vermes captures the significance of this moment for the disciples: "within a short time the terrified small group of the original followers of Jesus, still hiding from public gaze, all at once underwent a powerful mystical experience in Jerusalem on the Feast of Weeks (Pentecost). Filled with the promised Holy Spirit, the pusillanimous men were suddenly metamorphosed into ecstatic spiritual warriors." [84]

The Holy Spirit and the Great Outpouring

The coming of the Holy Spirit at Pentecost (referred to here as the Great Outpouring) is powerfully linked to the redemptive mission, plan and purpose of God, from Abraham to Jesus to us. Before delving into the significance of the event, a brief discussion of its locale may be in order.

Luke, the writer of Acts, mentions at the beginning of chapter two that the disciples were "all together in one place." Where was that place? Tradition refers to it as "the upper room" but this is not drawn explicitly from Scripture. While a detailed argument may be better suited elsewhere, suffice it to say that a convergence of evidence points to the

---

[84] Geza Vermes, *The Resurrection*, 149

Temple itself as the most likely location for the Great Outpouring. More specifically, the disciples may have gathered in an upstairs room adjacent to the Court of the Gentiles, where it is plausible that thousands of witnesses would be present.

Since the disciples in Jerusalem were, by and large, Jewish, the Temple is the only natural place for them to be at 9 in the morning, on the day of Shavu'ot. This is also the place where thousands of baptisms would naturally occur, at the Temple's ritual baths, or *mikvehs*.

Lest this question seem trivial, another look at Acts 2:2 may be in order, wherein the Spirit is described as filling "the whole house." It may indeed be a blessing for the Spirit to visit every room of a private residence (as western Christians often imagine it) but how much greater is it for the Spirit to be poured out on the Temple? Note that the Temple is often referred to in Scripture simply as "the House" and that tens of thousands of people routinely gathered there for Festival celebrations.

The scene of the Great Outpouring, described in the second chapter of Acts, centers around the baptism (or outpouring) of the Holy Spirit on the Jesus' disciples, and the welcome many new ones into the family of Believers. This purpose is especially fitting at such a time as Shavu'ot, when "there were staying in Jerusalem God-fearing Jews from every nation under heaven ... Parthians, Medes, Elamites, residents of Mesopotamia, Judea and Cappadocia, Pontus and Asia, Phrygia and Pamphylia, Egypt and parts of Libya near Cyrene; visitors from Rome (both Jews and converts to Judaism); Cretans and Arabs." [85]

---

[85] Acts 2:5, 9-11

This is essentially a description of the entire Jewish diaspora, stretching from Rome in the west to modern-day Iran in the east. (See map – permission pending)

THE NATIONS OF PENTECOST   ACTS 2:9-11

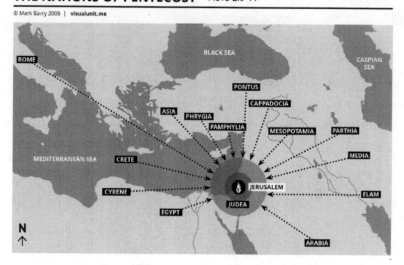

© Mark Barry 2009 | visualunit.me

What could have motivated the Jewish people in the Diaspora to travel such a distance to be present in Jerusalem for Shavu'ot? The journey, usually by foot, would have been long and difficult. Rome was over 1,400 miles as the crow flies, and many of the other places mentioned were over 600 miles away, so it would have taken a lot of time and money. Consequently, many travelers would have come for Passover and stayed through to Shavu'ot / Pentecost.

Acts 2:6 notes that these visitors each heard the disciples speak in their own language. It would have only been natural for the 3,000 devout Jews who were baptized that day to be share this message on their return journeys, and finally, in their home towns. [86] Thus, it was the diaspora Jews who took the good news message of the resurrected Jesus and the

---

[86] Edersheim, Sketches of Jewish Social Life, 46

fullness of the Spirit to the whole world. The initial message of the Gospel went forth even before the Apostles set out, and before Paul was even a disciple! There is no doubt that this was a sovereign work of God.

While there is some divergence amongst various Christian traditions regarding the interpretation of the concept of Holy Spirit Baptism, most agree that it was the promised gift of Jesus for the purpose of empowering the disciples for ministry.

With that, the series of events that had begun in the Temple over thirty years prior, when the angel Gabriel appeared to Zechariah were now complete. And, reaching further back, the desire of Moses' heart was fulfilled, when he wished that "all the Lord's people were prophets and that the Lord would put his Spirit on them." [87]

Pentecost Today

Pentecostal Christians, who get their name from the festival, often observe this time with a special emphasis on revivalism, and the individual experience of receiving the Holy Spirit. This is most regularly accompanied by the practice of speaking in tongues, or glossolalia/xenolalia, as depicted in Acts 2:4-11. Other expressions may include prophecy and divine healing. This is also true of some churches that identify as Charismatic.

Many western Christians who do not practice in this way still maintain vibrant traditions at Pentecost, especially those in the liturgical and sacramental denominations (Anglican, Lutheran, Methodist, Presbyterian, Roman Catholic, etc.)

While these expressions are far too diverse to enumerate here, some of the common ones include the wearing the color red (representing the tongues of fire above the disciples' heads) the symbol of the dove, for the Holy Spirit (as in Jesus' baptism in Matthew 3:16, Mark 1:10 and Luke 3:22) and the singing of hymns which focus on the Trinity and the Holy

---

[87] Geza Vermes, *The Resurrection*, 149 (includes quotation from Numbers 11:29)

Spirit.

While some traditions mark Pentecost as the "birthday of the Church", this perspective is of limited value. When one considers the festival's foundation in Shavu'ot, and the Church's rootedness in the covenants of Abraham, Moses and David, one must conclude that the "Church" (the Yahwistic community of believers in a divine messiah— whether past, present or future) stretches back much further than the year AD 30. Whether it began with Moses, or Abraham, or even Adam, however, is a question for another book.

When is Pentecost?

Much like Shavu'ot, Pentecost is tied in the western church calendar to the better-known festival which precedes it. Easter Sunday is the first day of the 50-day period called "Eastertide" (clearly intended to mirror the Jewish Counting of the Omer.) The 50th day of this period, then, is celebrated as Pentecost Sunday.

The earliest date on which Pentecost can occur on the Gregorian calendar is May 10. The latest is June 13.

12 Parallels between Shavu'ot and Pentecost

No doubt can remain that the Great Outpouring of the Holy Spirit occurred at the Jewish festival of Shavu'ot. But why? After Jesus ascended to heaven on the 40th day, why not send the Spirit right then? Why wait 10 more days? If we truly believe that God has a plan and a purpose then we must believe that it was not just a coincidence but there was some significance to the coming of the Spirit on Shavu'ot.

David Stern, translator of the *Complete Jewish Bible*, provides some historical background to Shavu'ot that helps to answer these questions. He writes in his Jewish New Testament Commentary: "[Because] it was

God's intention to bring the Jewish New Covenant [88] to the Jewish people in a Jewish way, he made maximal use of the Jewish festivals to convey new truths in ways that emphasized their connection with old truths. [89]

The new truths revealed in Passover and Shavu'ot were indeed connected to the old truths which would be explicitly shown by using God's appointed times as revealed to Moses over a thousand years prior. The revelation of the Holy Spirit was given within the revelation of the Feast of Weeks, as well as within the framework of all seven of the Levitical Festivals.

Thus, the association between Shavu'ot and the giving of the Law set the stage for the Great Outpouring of the Holy Spirit on Pentecost, as told in the second chapter of the book of Acts. The parallels between the two events are nothing less than astonishing, and those who understand the festival in both the Torah and in Acts can scarcely doubt that the two are tightly linked.

So here are the parallels we see between the two Holy Days, starting with the four elements of classical metaphysics: Earth, Wind, Fire and Water. These will be followed by a fifth element (or quintessence) which ties them together. After that, we'll look at some additional parallels that add meaning to the juxtaposition.

1) Earth

Shavu'ot, in its original form, is a festival celebrating the wheat harvest. Jewish people were expected to come to the Temple from every nation to make wave offerings of two loaves of bread. Since the quality of this produce was seen as a foreshadowing of the coming fall harvest, Shavu'ot was a time to declare hope and trust in the fullness of God's blessing. The two loaves served as a symbol of this.

Later (during the Second Temple period and beyond) the emphasis

---

[88] Jeremiah 31:30-33
[89] Stern, Jewish New Testament Commentary

shifted from a celebration of the harvest, to a commemoration of the giving of the Torah. Because Shavu'ot takes place seven weeks after Passover, it aligns in the Exodus story with the arrival of the nation of Israel at Mount Sinai. And because of what happened there, the mountain is revered as a holy place. As sacred earth. And when God arrived, that earth shook violently. (Exodus 19:18)

When the Holy Spirit was poured out on the Shavu'ot (Pentecost) after Yeshua's ascension, it happened at another elevated piece of sacred earth: the Temple Mount. Even though the Temple curtain had been torn in two just 50 days prior, God still chose this very specific place to begin his multi-lingual, multi-ethnic Messiah movement. And the result of the Spirit's arrival on that day? A great harvest of souls, as we'll explore below.

2) Wind (and Weather)

In both stories, of Mount Sinai in Exodus and the day of Pentecost in Acts, the weather played a major role. "In the morning of the third day, there was thunder and lightning, a thick cloud on the mountain, and the blast of an exceedingly loud shofar. All the people in the camp trembled." (Exodus 19:16) On the day of Pentecost, Luke writes that "suddenly there came from heaven a sound like a mighty rushing wind, and it filled the whole house where they were sitting." (Acts 2:2) Like a thunderclap in a horror movie, extreme weather is used to get the audience's attention. Something greater than us is happening here.

This sound of a violent wind or violent breath is often thought of as the evidence of the coming of the Holy Spirit (which, in Hebrew is *Ruach HaKodesh).* However, when a greater understanding of the meaning of *Ruach* may reveal that this was not simply evidence of the Spirit, but indeed the Spirit himself.

Ruach, which here is translated "Spirit", is the Hebrew word meaning "wind" or "breath". It is God's life-giving, sustaining energy which was explicitly active in the creation of the universe, and again in the creation of humankind. As in creation, the *Ruach* comes at Pentecost to animate that which is inert, and to harmonize that which is chaotic.

3) Fire

"Now the entire Mount Sinai was in smoke, because ADONAI had descended upon it in fire. The smoke ascended like the smoke of a furnace." (Exodus 19:18) Fire often serves as a sign of God's dramatic arrival, sometimes in judgment and sometimes in revelation.

The parallel with Pentecost is obvious, but the similarity makes the difference even more dramatic. At Mount Sinai, God arrived in a single massive inferno, like the eruption of a volcano that envelops the summit in smoke. At Pentecost, the fire was just as significant, but far gentler, and with a different message. Before, the point was to draw everyone's attention to the Almighty Creator, and his monolithic message to the new nation about to be birthed. But now, individual tongues of fire meant that individual children of God were being anointed with the divine authority to carry God's message to the nations.

4) Water

Water is a symbol of cleansing and purification, for obvious reasons. In preparation for God's revelation at Sinai, he has Moses "sanctify" the people, and instructs them to wash their clothes, in water of course. (Imagine how dirty they would be after walking fifty days through the desert.) So at Sinai the cleansing was a preparation for the people to receive the Torah from God, but at Pentecost, water came after the fact.

After the tongues of fire descended on the group of believers, and they spoke in many languages, Peter preached to the crowd.[90] When they responded with open hearts, he instructed them to "Repent, and let each of you be baptized [in water] in the name of Messiah Yeshua for the removal of your sins." (Acts 2:38)

---

[90] If Pentecost is the reflection of Shavu'ot, it is here that Peter becomes the reflection of Moses.

5) Word (the Quintessence)

The four elements were the foundation of classical metaphysics for centuries before Aristotle introduced a fifth element (or "quintessence", which he called "aether") to serve as a source and a culmination of the first four. If believers were looking for a symbol that gives rise to all other symbols, surely it would be the Word. It is by the Word of God that light and the universe came to be, and by the Word that is Yeshua that all those created in his image might be rescued from darkness.

Despite the theatrics surrounding Mount Sinai, the ultimate purpose of the encounter was to receive a Word from God. What sets this apart from all other prophetic words, is that God etched them into stone with his own finger. (Exodus 31:18) What would you give to see a sample of God's penmanship?

The Word was also at the very center of the day of Pentecost. Although this time, like with the fire, it served a very different purpose. Instead of a single epic message spoken through a single prophet, it was divided into every language, to speak of the mighty deeds of God to every tribe who had traveled to worship at the Temple. Although they came from every corner of the globe, the people were all there for one reason: to commemorate the giving of the Torah. With that in mind, which "mighty deeds" might the believers have proclaimed in those diverse tongues?

Other Parallels

6) **Culmination.** Although Passover is the most significant holiday in the Jewish calendar, it is just the beginning of a journey that leads to Shavu'ot, and the giving of the Torah. And just as Holy Week is at the heart of the Church calendar, it culminates in Pentecost, which gives birth to a new global community of Believers.

7) **Counting to 50.** Shavu'ot is the Hebrew word for "weeks" referring to the seven weeks after Passover, leading up to the Feast of Shavu'ot, which was the next day. This is called the Counting of the Omer.

Pentecost is the Greek word for "50th" to indicate the final day of the "50 days of Easter". (It's worth noting that "Eastertide" technically begins on the evening before Easter day, which is another reflection of its origins in the Jewish calendar.)

8) Sunday. According to the Sadducees, the Counting of the Omer begins after the first Sabbath day of Passover. That means that the 50th day of the count will always fall on the first day of the week, or Sunday. Likewise, Pentecost is always exactly seven weeks after Easter, meaning that it falls on a Sunday every year as well. And since the first day of the week is symbolic of new beginnings...

9) New Religion. Many scholars view Mount Sinai as the birthplace of Judaism, and Pentecost as the birthplace of Christianity. Both occur on the first day of the week, a time for new beginnings.

10) Law. Shavu'ot commemorates God writing the Law (Torah) on stone, and Pentecost is the time when the Spirit of God wrote that Law on our hearts.

God used the great outpouring at Pentecost both to reflect the momentous scene where the Law is given, and to unravel the effects of sin, which is something the Law can never do. That's why we see some of these parallels affirming the Shavu'ot tradition, and other parallels appearing to fulfill it, wrap it up, and/or start something new.

11) Trumpet. "[There was] the blast of an exceedingly loud *shofar*[91] ... When the sound of the shofar grew louder and louder, Moses spoke, and God answered him with a thunderous sound." (Exodus 19:16,19)

At Mount Sinai, the shofar (ram's horn, or trumpet) began at "exceedingly loud" volume and then got louder and louder. I believe "ear-splitting" would be an appropriate adjective here. The Israelites were to make no mistake that this was God was speaking, and not Moses.

At Pentecost, Luke makes it clear that the outpouring takes place at precisely 9 in the morning. (or the "third hour") Whenever Scripture is

---

[91] *Shofar:* Trumpet or Ram's horn

specific about the time of day, there's always a reason. What is the reason in this case? Because the morning Temple sacrifice occurred every day at the third hour, accompanied by the sound of a *shofar*.

12) 3,000 People. Exodus 32:28 recounts, "So the sons of Levi did as Moses said, and that day from among the people there fell about 3,000 men." Acts 2:41 recounts, "So those who received his message were baptized, and that day about 3,000 souls were added."

Both of these verses start with the word "so", meaning they are a result of what came before. Because the followers of Moses were unfaithful and put their trust in an idol, about 3,000 people died. And because the followers of Yeshua were faithful and trusted God for "power from on high", they received that power, and 3,000 people were saved.

Conclusion

Although Priscilla's story takes place thirty-two years after the Great Outpouring (or the first Christian Pentecost, estimated to have occurred in AD 30) it serves to echo this milestone in the fictional events set forth in first-century Ephesus.

While we, as Believers, should not expect the Acts of the Apostles to repeat themselves in our own time, we should nevertheless look to the Holy Spirit to move in transformative ways in our own lives.

In other words, Shavu'ot / Pentecost is more than a past event, and more than an annual festival. Rather, it is an unbroken reality for all who trust the Spirit of God to renew their hearts day by day.

Hebrew Terms

ADONAI (ah-doh-NAI): LORD. Used as a substitute for the name given to Moses at the burning bush.

Omer (OH-mare), **counting of**: The marking of the fifty days (seven weeks plus one) after Passover, leading to the celebration of *Shavu'ot.*

Seder (SAY-der): Literally, "order"; usually referring to the ceremonial Passover meal itself. There are many different Seder traditions.

Shavu'ot (shah-voo-OTE): The Feast of Weeks; a spring wheat-harvest festival that marks the end of the Counting of the Omer.

Sukkah (SOO-kuh): A small structure built as a temporary dwelling for the celebration of *Sukkot.* Observant Jews sleep in these at night, with a view of the stars, for the duration of the holiday.

Sukkot (soo-KOTE): The eight-day long Feast of Tabernacles; the seventh of God's appointed times as outlined in Leviticus 23. Some experts have concluded that Jesus was born during *Sukkot.*

Torah (TORE-ah): "Law". The first five books of the Bible. Also known as the "Law of Moses" or the Pentateuch.

Yeshua (yeh-SHOO-ah): Jesus' Hebrew name; what his relatives and peers would have called him. Literally, "Salvation" or "God Saves."

Key Scriptures

Counting of the Omer, Shavu'ot and Pentecost
Tree of Life Version (TLV)

From the Hebrew Scriptures

Exodus 34:22

You are to observe the Feast of Shavu'ot, which is the firstfruits of the wheat harvest, as well as the Feast of Ingathering at the turn of the year.

Leviticus 23:15-21

Then you are to count from the morrow after the *Shabbat*,[92] from the day that you brought the omer of the wave offering, seven complete *Shabbatot*. Until the morrow after the seventh Shabbat you are to count fifty days, and then present a new grain offering to ADONAI.

You are to bring out of your houses two loaves of bread for a wave offering, made of two tenths of an ephah of fine flour. They are to be baked with hametz as firstfruits to ADONAI. You are to present, along with the bread, seven one-year-old lambs without blemish, one young bull, and two rams. They will become a burnt offering to ADONAI, with their meal offering, and their drink offerings, an offering made by fire, a sweet aroma to ADONAI. Also you are to offer one male goat for a sin offering and a pair of year-old male lambs for a sacrifice of fellowship offerings. The kohen is to wave them with the bread of the firstfruits as a wave offering before ADONAI, with the two lambs. They should be holy to ADONAI for the kohen. You are to make a proclamation on the same day that there is to be a holy convocation, and you shall do no regular work.

---

[92] *Shabbat* is the Hebrew word for Sabbath. *Shabbatot* is the plural.

This is a statute forever in all your dwellings throughout your generations.

Deuteronomy 16:9-12

Seven weeks you are to count for yourself—from the time you begin to put the sickle to the standing grain you will begin to count seven weeks. Then you will keep the Feast of Shavu'ot to ADONAI your God with a measure of a freewill offering from your hand, which you are to give according to how ADONAI your God blesses you. So you will rejoice before ADONAI your God in the place ADONAI your God chooses to make His Name dwell—you, your son and daughter, slave and maid, Levite and outsider, orphan and widow in your midst. You will remember that you were a slave in Egypt, and you are to take care and do these statutes.

Joel 2:13 – 3:5

Rend your heart, not your garments, and turn to ADONAI, your God. For He is gracious and compassionate, slow to anger, abundant in mercy, and relenting about the calamity due. Who knows? He may turn and relent, and may leave a blessing behind Him—so there may be a grain offering and a drink offering for ADONAI, your God.

Blow the *shofar*[93] in Zion! Sanctify a fast; proclaim an assembly. Gather the people; sanctify the congregation; assemble the elders; gather the children, even those nursing at breasts. Let the bridegroom come out from his bedroom and the bride from her chamber. Between the porch and the altar let the *kohanim,*[94] ministers of ADONAI, weep, and let them say: "Have pity, ADONAI, on Your people. Don't make Your heritage a scorn, a byword among the nations. Why should the peoples say, 'Where is their God?'" ADONAI will be zealous for His land, and have compassion on His people. ADONAI will answer and say to His people: "Behold, I will send you the grain, the new wine, and the fresh oil, and you will be

---

[93] Ram's horn
[94] Priests

satisfied with it. I will no longer make you a mockery among the nations.

"But I will remove the northern invader far from you—yes, I will banish him to a dry and desolate land— his vanguard into the Eastern Sea and his rearguard into the Western Sea. His odor will go up— Yes, his stench will rise." For He has done great things!

Do not fear, O land. Be glad! Rejoice! For ADONAI has done great things. Do not be afraid, beasts of the field, for the desert pastures have sprouted, for the tree bears its fruit. Fig tree and vine yield their strength. So be glad, children of Zion, and rejoice in ADONAI, your God. For He gives you the early rain for prosperity, Yes, He will bring down rain for you, the early and latter rain as before.

The threshing floors will be full of grain and the vats will overflow with new wine and fresh oil. "I shall restore to you the years that the locust, the swarming locust, the canker-worm and the caterpillar have eaten— My great army that I sent among you.

You will surely eat and be satisfied, and praise the Name of ADONAI your God, who has dealt wondrously with you. Never again will My people be shamed. You will know that I am within Israel. Yes, I am ADONAI your God—there is no other—Never again will My people be shamed.

"So it will be afterward, I will pour out My *Ruach*[95] on all flesh: your sons and daughters will prophesy, your old men will dream dreams, your young men will see visions. Also on the male and the female servants will I pour out My spirit in those days.

I will show wonders in the heavens and on the earth—blood, fire and pillars of smoke. The sun will be turned into darkness and the moon into blood, before the great and awesome day of ADONAI comes. Then all who call on ADONAI's Name will escape, for on Mount Zion and in Jerusalem there will be rescue, as ADONAI has said, among the survivors whom ADONAI is calling."

---

[95] Spirit

From the New Testament

Luke 24:44-49

Then He said to them, "These are My words which I spoke to you while I was still with you—everything written concerning Me in the Torah of Moses and the Prophets and the Psalms must be fulfilled.

Then He opened their minds to understand the Scriptures, and He said to them, "So it is written, that the Messiah is to suffer and to rise from the dead on the third day, and that repentance for the removal of sins is to be proclaimed in His name to all nations, beginning from Jerusalem. You are witnesses of these things.

And behold, I am sending the promise of My Father upon you; but you are to stay in the city until you are clothed with power from on high."

Acts 1:4-5

Now while staying with them, He commanded them not to leave Jerusalem, but to wait for what the Father promised—which, He said, "you heard from Me. For John immersed with water, but you will be immersed in the *Ruach ha-Kodesh* not many days from now."

Acts 2:1-21

When the day of Shavu'ot had come, they were all together in one place. Suddenly there came from heaven a sound like a mighty rushing wind, and it filled the whole house where they were sitting. And tongues like fire spreading out appeared to them and settled on each one of them. They were all filled with the *Ruach ha-Kodesh* and began to speak in other tongues as the *Ruach* enabled them to speak out. Now Jewish people were staying in Jerusalem, devout men from every nation under heaven.

And when this sound came, the crowd gathered. They were bewildered, because each was hearing them speaking in his own language. And they were amazed and astonished, saying, "All these who are speaking—aren't they Galileans? How is it that we each hear our own birth language? Parthians and Medes and Elamites and those living in Mesopotamia, Judea and Cappadocia, Pontus and Asia, Phrygia and Pamphylia, Egypt and parts of Libya toward Cyrene, and visitors from Rome (both Jewish people and proselytes), Cretans and Arabs—we hear them declaring in our own tongues the mighty deeds of God!"

And they were all amazed and perplexed, saying to each other, "What does this mean?" Others, poking fun, were saying, "They are full of sweet new wine!"

But Peter, standing with the Eleven, raised his voice and addressed them: "Fellow Judeans and all who are staying in Jerusalem, let this be known to you, and pay attention to my words. These men are not drunk, as you suppose—for it's only the third hour of the day! But this is what was spoken about through the prophet Joel: 'And it shall be in the last days,' says God, 'that I will pour out My *Ruach* on all flesh. Your sons and your daughters shall prophesy, your young men shall see visions, and your old men shall dream dreams. Even on My slaves, male and female, I will pour out My *Ruach* in those days, and they shall prophesy.

And I will give wonders in the sky above and signs on the earth beneath— blood, and fire, and smoky vapor. The sun shall be turned to darkness and the moon to blood before the great and glorious Day of ADONAI comes. And it shall be that everyone who calls on the name of ADONAI shall be saved.'

Resources

Bibliography and Recommended Books

Bailey, Kenneth E. *Jesus Through Middle Eastern Eyes: Cultural Studies in the Gospels.* Downers Grove: IVP Academic, 2008.

Beale, G.K. and D.A. Carson, ed. *Commentary on the New Testament use of the Old Testament.* Grand Rapids: Baker Academic, 2007.

Edersheim, Alfred. *Sketches of Jewish Social Life.* Peabody: Hendrickson Publishers, 1994.

Edersheim, Alfred. *The Life and Times of Jesus the Messiah.* Peabody: Hendrickson Publishers, 1886.

Edersheim, Alfred. *The Temple: Its Ministry and Services As They Were at the Time of Jesus Christ.* Grand Rapids: Eerdmans, 1992.

Finto, Don. *Your People Shall Be My People: Expanded Edition.* Chosen Books, 2016.

Hagner, Donald A. *The Jewish Reclamation of Jesus: An Analysis and Critique of the Modern Jewish Study of Jesus.* Grand Rapids: Zondervan, 1984.

Hoppin, Ruth. *Priscilla's Letter: Finding the Author of the Epistle to the Hebrews.* Fort Bragg, California: Lost Coast Press, 2000.

Jeremias, Joachim. *Jerusalem in the Time of Jesus.* Philadelphia: Fortress Press, 1962.

Juster, Dan. *Jewish Roots: Understanding Your Jewish Faith.* Gaithersburg: Davar Publishing, 2013.

Kaiser, Walter C. Jr. *Mission in the Old Testament: Israel as a Light to the Nations*. Grand Rapids: Baker Academic, 2000.

Kasdan, Barney. *God's Appointed Times*. Clarksville: Messianic Jewish Publishers, 1993.

Keener, Craig S. *The Historical Jesus of the Gospels*. Grand Rapids: Eerdmans, 2009.

Keener, Craig S. *The IVP Bible Background Commentary: New Testament*. Grand Rapids: Eerdmans, 1993.

Keener, Craig S. *Romans: A New Covenant Commentary*. Eugene: Cascade: 2009.

Lapide, Pinchas. *The Resurrection of Jesus: a Jewish Perspective*. Minneapolis: Augsburg, 1983.

Lightfoot, John. *A Commentary on the New Testament from the Talmud and Hebraica: Volume 4*. Peabody: Hendrickson Publishers, 1979.

Prager, Dennis, and Joseph Telushkin, ed., *The Rational Bible: Exodus: God, Slavery, and Freedom*. Washington, D.C., Regnery Faith, 2018.

Rosen, Moishe and Ceil Rosen. *Christ in the Passover*. Chicago: Moody Press, 2006.

Sarna, Nahum M. "Exodus" *The JPS Torah Commentary*, edited by Nahum M. Sarna and Chaim Potok. Jerusalem: The Jewish Publication Society, 1989.

Seif, Jeffrey L. "Yeshua and Israel in the Third Millennium." The King's University, 2011.

Skarsaune, Oskar. *In the Shadow of the Temple*. Downers Grove: InterVarsity Press, 2002.

Stein, Robert H. *The Method and Message of Jesus' Teaching*. Philadelphia: The Westminster Press, 1978.

Stern, David H. *Complete Jewish Bible*. Clarksville: Jewish New Testament Publications, 1998.

Stern, David H. *Jewish New Testament Commentary*. Clarksville: Jewish New Testament Publications, 1992.

Stern, David H. *Messianic Judaism: A Modern Movement With an Ancient Past*. Clarksville: Jewish New Testament Publications, 2013.

Vermes, Geza. *The Resurrection*. New York: Doubleday, 2008.

Wilson, Marvin. *Our Father Abraham: Jewish Roots of the Christian Faith*. Grand Rapids: Eerdmans, 1989.

Books by Jim Jacob

To learn more about Yeshua the Messiah, we recommend three books by Jim Jacob. You can read them for free online at www.jimjacobbooks.com/read-for-free, or purchase a printed copy.

A Lawyer's Case for the Resurrection offers historical and logical evidence for the Resurrection of Jesus, including documentation from Jewish sources and others who do not believe Jesus was the Messiah.

A Lawyer's Case for God offers evidence for the existence of God and the validity of the Bible. It also addresses topics such as: the problem with organized religion, the myth of being a "good person", that the idea that Jews don't believe in Jesus, and whether the Bible is, in fact, outdated.

A Lawyer's Case for His Faith builds on A Lawyer's Case for God and also explores topics such as: the existence of a good God in a world filled with suffering, the idea that all religions can be correct, whether the bible and science can be reconciled, and the identity of Jesus as the Jewish Messiah.

Bibles & Commentaries

Complete Jewish Bible (CJB). Clarksville: Jewish New Testament Publications, 1998.

Complete Jewish Study Bible. Clarksville: Jewish New Testament Publications, 2016.

Sarna, Nahum P., ed. *JPS Torah Commentary: Exodus*. Jerusalem: Jewish Publication Society, 1991.

Stern, David H. *Jewish New Testament Commentary*. Clarksville: Jewish New Testament Publications, 1992.

The Holy Bible, *Tree of Life Version (TLV)*. Grand Rapids: Baker Books, 2015.

Websites

OurFatherAbraham.com

Devoted to the purpose of educating followers and admirers of Jesus about the Hebraic context of the good news, and the centrality of the Jewish festivals to the Christian faith.

MessianicJewish.net

Reaching out to Jewish people with the message of Messiah and teaching our non-Jewish spiritual family about their Jewish roots.

Hebrew4Christians.com

An excellent resource for those interested in Hebrew. The vision is to provide a resource for the Church regarding its rich Hebraic heritage by promoting Jewish literacy among all those who believe in Jesus.

ThatTheWorldMayKnow.com

The ministry website of Ray VanderLaan is focused on understanding the Bible in light of the historical and cultural context in which God placed it. The platform is rich in both biblical insight and media content, featuring audio, video and text lessons.

Primary Messianic Organizations

There are many Messianic Jewish and Messianic Gentile organizations (non-profit and congregational). Following are several of the primary organizations along with their vision statements, according to their websites.

Tikkun International (www.tikkunministries.org)

Tikkun International is a Messianic Jewish umbrella organization for an apostolic network of leaders, congregations and ministries in covenantal relationship for mutual accountability, support and equipping to extend the Kingdom of God in America, Israel, and throughout the world.

Messianic Jewish Alliance of America (mjaa.org)

Founded in 1915, the MJAA is the largest association of Messianic Jewish and non-Jewish believers in Yeshua (Hebrew for Jesus) in the world. Its purpose is threefold: (1) to testify to the large and growing number of Jewish people who believe that Yeshua is the promised Jewish Messiah and Savior of the world, (2) to bring together Jewish and non-Jewish people who have a shared vision for Jewish revival, and, most importantly (3) to introduce their Jewish brothers and sisters to the Jewish Messiah Yeshua.

International Alliance of Messianic Congregations and Synagogues (www.iamcs.org)

The spiritual vision of the IAMCS is to see the outpouring of God's Spirit upon Jewish people through Messianic congregations. The IAMCS is not designed to be a denominational structure, but rather to be an instrument in promoting Messianic revival and to provide for the needs of its members, whatever their affiliations.

Union of Messianic Jewish Congregations (www.umjc.org)

The UMJC is a network of over 75 congregations in 8 countries. Together, they establish and grow Jewish congregations that honor Yeshua, the Messiah of Israel. For nearly 40 years, the Union has provided a venue for mutual support, lively debate, joint activism, and practical leadership development.

About the Authors

Lon A. Wiksell, D.Min.

Originally from Sioux City, Iowa, Lon grew up in church as the son of Pentecostal pastors. He completed his first two years of college in Iowa before moving to Springfield Missouri and working for Evangel University where he met his wife Fran. He later worked for Drury University and Missouri State University, where he also completed his BS and MBA. After working for Phillips Petroleum Company in Bartlesville, Oklahoma he moved the family to Tulsa in 1988, to study at Oral Roberts University. He received his M.Div. from there in 1992. After graduating they moved to Kansas City where they became involved in the Messianic Jewish movement. In 2013 he received his Doctorate of Ministry in Messianic Jewish Studies from The King's University.

Lon and Fran were co-founders and co-leaders of Or HaOlam Messianic Congregation from 1995 to 2002. They then went on to start House of Messiah in 2004, devoted to understanding the words of Yeshua within their historical context and celebrating the seven biblical festivals as a pattern of personal and community life. House of Messiah has now merged with Kingdom Living Messianic Congregation, and Lon and Fran are now highly involved in organizing city-wide biblical festivals.

Ryan Wiksell

Ryan was raised in the Assemblies of God in Northeastern Oklahoma, and joined the Messianic Jewish movement with his family in Kansas City during his high school years. A personal call to ministry then led him to study music and theology at Evangel University.

Doors were then opened for him to serve in various Southern Baptist churches, where he held positions in music leadership and communications. Ryan married Christina in 2003, and shortly thereafter they pursued a call to plant a grassroots independent church in downtown Springfield, MO, called The Front Porch. After this effort drew to a close in 2011, they sought out a new spiritual family, which they found in Christ Episcopal Church in Springfield.

Today, Ryan and Christina are blessed to be the parents of twin four-year-olds Asher and Anya. Ryan and his family are currently residing in Alexandria, Virginia, while he is enrolled in the Master of Divinity program at Virginia Theological Seminary.